BLOOD KIN

Woods's men skittered off the street and darted through the deserted ruins.

"They're going to get away!" Mamudi exclaimed.

Crazy Jack said, "Naaaah."

From the distance came the familiar sound of Kinski's AK-47. A minute later Kinski strode out from the ruins.

Jack said, "Any survivors?"

"Are you kidding?" Kinski asked.

THE MARAUDERS

CAPTAIN "CRAZY JACK" KEENAN—The ultimate warrior, he doesn't need a weapon. He is a weapon.

SERGEANT CHAN—A deadly marksman who never misses.

CPO FREDDIE MAMUDI—A knife-wielding Afghan freedom fighter.

LIEUTENANT KINSKI—A human death machine who rocks-and-rolls with an assault rifle instead of a guitar.

THE MARAUDERS series
from Jove

THE MARAUDERS
BLOOD KIN

LIAR'S DICE
(Coming in February)

THE MARAUDERS
BLOOD KIN

MICHAEL McGANN

JOVE BOOKS, NEW YORK

THE MARAUDERS: BLOOD KIN

A Jove Book / published by arrangement with
the author

PRINTING HISTORY
Jove edition / December 1989

ISBN: 0-515-10208-3

Jove Books are published by The Berkley Publishing Group,
200 Madison Avenue, New York, New York 10016.
The name "JOVE" and the "J" logo
are trademarks belonging to Jove Publications, Inc.

PRINTED IN THE UNITED STATES OF AMERICA

10 9 8 7 6 5 4 3 2 1

In memory of
Frances Glazener

ONE

Captain John F. "Crazy Jack" Keenan wrapped his massive frame around a small chair in a London pub. His back ached. His head ached. His heart ached. He ordered another gin and tonic, allowing himself to surrender to the effect of the last six he had ordered. Under no circumstances did he want to think straight.

He rubbed a smooth hand through his tangle of red hair. He stared at his right hand. Once it had been callused. Now it was suffering from inactivity.

It was smooth and lazy.

What the hell was he doing over here, anyway, so far away from home?

Home? He laughed to himself. There was no more "home" as he had come to know it. The United States, before the big nuke-out, had been his home.

But it was gone now.

And most of his memories had evaporated with it.

Now he felt as much of an endangered species as the bison.

"Bison," he said aloud, and laughed, causing some of the old men at the bar to turn his way.

"What are you looking at?" Jack snapped. "Haven't you ever seen a hero before?"

He was a hero, and everybody knew it. Still, that offered no comfort to Keenan. His very soul ached with a phrase he could never complete: "I want . . . I want . . ."

He began to laugh again, a whistling, almost howling sound. He was losing it. And losing it quickly.

He had a family once. But they had been reduced to ashes back on the East Coast. New Jersey. Still too hot a spot to explore.

He had been a Green Beret captain with a few tours in Nicaragua to his credit. A six-foot-four bull of a man, he had once cultivated his mind. He had a combined M.S. in chemistry and physics and had even written a few books on New Age physics.

He wasn't an asshole.

So why did he feel like one?

He felt like one because he had no roots. Nothing to go back to. Nothing to look forward to. For the last four or five months he had been employed by the current United States President, Jeffrey MacGregor, to mastermind the unshackling of Western Europe, currently in the hands of a government called the Federated States of Europe. The kind of sprawling mind-set last seen when Hitler was wooing Europe before the Second World War.

He was part of a guerrilla outfit called the Marauders. Five men hired to fight impossible odds and plant the seeds of freedom around the Continent.

Four men now.

Tom Bee, their Hopi guru and one hell of a fighter, had gone up like a matchstick in their first operation.

Crazy Jack grimaced. He should be used to this kind of stuff by now.

In a way he was. What he wasn't used to was sitting on his ass for prolonged periods of time. Which was what he was doing now.

And so he drank.

And when he was done, he drank some more.

He didn't quite know what it was all about, what was going on in his mind. He turned to no one in particular. "In the classical Newtonian view of 'I,'" he began, "'I' is primarily an observer—of reality."

He downed his new drink and ordered another. "In the Quantum view, 'I' is a participant. Reality is a function of my interaction with an infinite number of possibilities.

"Ah, but the Involvement view has 'I' as a separation of consciousness and can participate with action! Action!"

He banged the table with his fist. "Action!" he repeated. "That's what I need. In physics, the path of least action is known as ordinary reality. I am now ordinary. I am taking the path of least action."

That was the problem. How can you train a man to be a fighter, a soldier, a strategist and then keep him in cold storage for months?

It seemed easier for the other Marauders. Gunnery Sergeant Winston S. "Buddha" Chan took great delight in teaching the newly re-formed British Army and RAF gangs martial arts and sharpshooting skills. He had been known as the best sniper in the Marine Corps before the big nuke-out.

Navy SEAL Freddie Mamudi, when not delving into libraries to relish books on his Sunni Muslim beliefs, took great delight in showing any female who would look twice his collections of glass eyes (the right one was blown out by a Soviet sniper) and his Zipper. That's what Freddie called the long scar that ran from his hairline to his glass eye, for obvious reasons. Since Freddie's religion encouraged multiple wives, Freddie had spent his recent downtime seeking out as many as he could get his hands on. And for a man of his thin, wiry build, he had very large hands.

One strange thing about Mamudi, though. Since the death of Tom Bee, whom Freddie had considered a true spiritual leader, Mamudi had seemed to grow more religious, in the classical sense of the word. He had become less outgoing. More introspective. More prone to philosophizing. Sure, Jack still regarded him as a blabbering idiot, but now his idiocy was better phrased. More spiritual somehow. It was as if Tom Bee had tossed a hefty amount of luggage at Mamudi's feet, and now Freddie was in the midst of constantly unpacking it.

Lieutenant Peter Kinski, USAF, had been coaching the new RAF boys both in flying whatever crates they could get their hands on (the last World War had decimated most of the flying craft in Europe, since all air bases were on the first-strike list) and finding whatever women they could do likewise with. Skinny and suave, Kinski loved women as much as Freddie did, but he wasn't as enamored with the thought of marriage.

Kinski loved women almost as much as he did his hair, which was done in the classic fifties pompadour style. If it wasn't for its straw color and Kinski's aversion to leather, he could have been called Fonzi.

And that left Crazy Jack. He still loved his wife, although she had been dead for years. He still missed his kids, who'd perished in their mother's arms, Jack hoped. He hated to think of the kids dying somewhere on their own. Wide-eyed. Terrified.

Awestruck by the white light, white heat.

He ordered another drink.

All he could do now was fight. Fight and kill. Kill who? The bad guys. There were always bad guys. He was thankful to the president for giving him a laundry list of thugs to pursue throughout Europe.

But transatlantic communication was difficult these days. Sometimes it took weeks or even months to get a message through.

Across the great Atlantic.

So he sat while ex-cop King Shatterhand—a big, bearded fellow for whom the Marauders had saved England—tried his best to pull both England and Scotland into shape.

So Jack sat drinking.

Thinking about things long behind.

And trying to figure out what he was doing with his life.

"I'd like another," he said, motioning to the barmaid.

"I think you've had enough, sir," the tiny brown-haired woman said.

"You know what?" Crazy Jack replied. "You look like a mouse."

He cackled. "That's it. A mouse. M-O-U-S-E. Ha! How do you like that!"

The barmaid ran for the owner. "You're not very funny, Yank."

"I haven't done my John Wayne imitation yet. Guaranteed to break the ice at parties."

The room regarded him in silence.

"Great. I come all the way from America to help free you folks, get you a new king, and I wind up dealing with the deaf-mute chorus of London."

Crazy Jack lifted his two hundred and twenty pounds out of the Lilliputian chair and ambled over to the bar. A small fat man was doing the bartending.

"Duck," Jack said, leaning over the bar.

The barkeep did as he was told. Jack took a bottle of gin and began to guzzle it.

"Tell you what," he said, addressing the crowd in the tavern. "I'll buy ten free drinks for anyone who can arm-wrestle me! Whaddaya say?"

"Sod off."

"Piss off."

"Sleep it off, Yank."

Crazy Jack frowned, sending his craggy features into something resembling a portrait of Quasimodo. "Hey! I'm on R and R here! Come on, who wants to arm-wrassle?"

Jack stood there. The room began to swim. He shouldn't have had that last drink. No, that wasn't it. He shouldn't have guzzled that last bottle.

He heard police whistles in the background.

"Shit," he hissed.

The mouse had called the cops. These days, the London police were fully armed. Standard-issue Colt .45s. Mini-Uzis when they were called for. They were tougher these days as well. Not quite so polite as before the war. Jack guessed that having your country subjugated could have something to do with it.

He stood, weaving at the bar, as six English bobbies entered the pub.

"What's the problem?" the lead boy in blue demanded.

"No one wants to arm-wrestle," Jack explained.

The lead bobby made a move for Jack. Jack straightened himself immediately.

Action.

A second bobby whispered something to the first. The first bobby nodded. "Oh, it's you, Captain Keenan. We have orders, if we were to run across you, to take you home safely . . . under police escort."

Jack thought about this and nodded. "Piss up a rope. I have no home."

"Now come along quietly, then," the first bobby said, extending a hand.

Before he knew it, the cop had sailed through the pub's front window, landing with a thud on the ground outside in a shower of broken glass.

Jack stood before the bar. "Who's next, you ... you ... *cops,* you!"

The five police dived at Jack as one. Jack let out a war whoop and began flailing away at them with his massive fists. He felt a nose break. An arm pop out of joint. There went a knee. Two ribs here. Three ribs there.

As he tossed the police around the pub like Superballs, he heard more police whistles. He still had a few seconds.

"Give me another drink, beautiful," he said, tossing a handful of five-pound notes the mousy barmaid's way. "Did I ever tell you how much you look like a very young Elizabeth Taylor?"

She grinned at him and the money.

"A drink you want, is it? Aye, aye, Captain." She smiled. "And I've always considered you an *orange* Douglas Fairbanks."

"I wished you'd have told me that an hour earlier," Jack said, wheezing.

The waitress grinned.

She tossed him a full bottle of gin. He downed it.

Jack turned to the crowd. "How about a drink in honor of the late, great Roy Orbison. You remember him, don't you?"

Jack took a deep breath and attempted to sing. "'Only the lonely ... know the way I feel tonight.'"

No response.

"Come on, it was my wife's favorite song."

The door of the pub burst open.

Jack saw a flash of blue.

He took a deep breath.

Ten minutes and thirty bobbies later, Jack found himself trussed up in the back of a police van, screaming on the way to Scotland Yard.

"Jesus Mortimer Christ!" he bellowed. "Can't you keep that racket down? I have a headache."

He felt the van clatter to a stop.

Jack, shackled, was led past the booking desk at Scotland Yard. "Hello, Inspector Munru, Sergeant Kinnard, Patrolman Sellers."

"Hello, Jack," they muttered.

Inspector Munru, a portly man with an always sweaty brow, waddled up to Jack. "I'm afraid you've done it this time, Jackie."

"Awww, Inspector," Jack said, "give me a break."

"We have, Jackie, many's the time. But now I'm afraid we're going to have to prosecute. You've sent twenty-six men to hospital this time."

"They fought bravely, Inspector."

The inspector sighed. "I know they did, Jackie. But frankly, we're running out of patrolmen for you to play with."

"Can't you give them medals or something and just let me go?"

"And where will you go this time?"

Jack's face fell. "Exactly what I was thinking. Okay. Lock me up, then."

Jack allowed himself to be led into a small cell. He stretched out on the brick-hard cot and went to sleep. Rather, it was a state of welcome unconsciousness.

When he awoke, he heard a commotion in the hall.

Jack raised his massive frame up and found himself staring at King Shatterhand, formerly Willis MacGregor, distant cousin to Jack's own president.

MacGregor was as big as Jack, with hair just as red but accompanied by a full, bushy beard and a mangled left hand encased in a studded leather glove. The hair and beard were gifts of his parents. The mangled hand was the gift of the Federated States of Europe.

Shatterhand sighed. "Jack, what are we going to do with you?"

"Beats me, Your Highness." Jack shrugged.

"You've been in your cups for weeks now."

"Ten and a half weeks." Jack grinned. "But who's counting?"

"What's your problem, Jack? The other Marauders have taken to the lull quite nicely. What can we do to calm you down?"

"Send me somewhere to *fight,* goddammit," Jack said. "That's what I'm here for. That's what I *do*."

"We have to bide our time."

"Great," Jack said. "That's just like you British."

"I'm a Scot!"

"You're a *cripple,*" Jack snapped, hating himself for saying it. "The Scots rolled over for the British. The British rolled over for the FSE. You wouldn't see Americans letting some foreign assholes take us over. That's what I'm here for, to show some American spunk. Get me out of here. Drop me in any country. I'll kick FSE ass."

"That's the liquor talking."

"That's Captain John F. Keenan talking. Listen, Mac-Gregor, you *need* me. Don't ever forget that. And if you don't think you need me now, just wait a couple a days or so and look over your shoulder. They'll be some FSE asshole ready to take you out. And who'll protect you? Your fuggin' little bobbies with their fire-hydrant helmets and guns they can barely fire? No! It'll be Jack Keenan, that's who.

"Jack Keenan! Don't you ever forget that!"

King Shatterhand gritted his teeth. "That's it, Jack. I wash my hands of you."

"*Hand,* Your Highness." Jack smirked, sinking back down on his cot.

The king stormed out of the jail, leaving a seething Jack behind. "There's not a jail in this pansy country of yours that can hold Crazy Jack fuggin' Keenan!" Jack roared.

He got up out of his cot and charged headfirst into the cell's bars.

Much to his amazement, they didn't give way.

His head did.

He sank to the ground.

Inspector Munru ran in. "Jackie? Jackie?"

"Oh, ossifer," Jack called, "would you mind taking me to a hospital?"

"What?"

Jack felt his eyelids flutter and his spine shrivel. "I think I have concussed myself."

His consciousness swam.

He hit the cell floor with a thud.

The next thing he knew, he was staring into the face of a young nun. "Mother of Mercy," he whispered, "have I gone to heaven?"

"No," the nun said. "St. Mary's."

"Close enough," Jack said, passing out. And in his dreams he was with his wife and children again.

He was a whole man. A whole "I."

And in the deepest valley of his soul he felt good about that.

TWO

Ian O'Malley directed his driver to turn right down a countrified street in the Northern Irish town of Feirgall. "It's right up ahead," the short wiry man said.

"Yes, sir," his driver, a fellow named Mike, replied. He was a local lad and hadn't much brains, but he knew the territory.

O'Malley enjoyed being called sir these days. As a favored lackey of Chairman Yevgeny Maximov, Supreme Leader of the Federated States of Europe, he was well beyond his old drug-dealing, gunrunning, and pimping days.

Well, not *that* beyond it all. He was still dealing with all three areas of endeavor, but now it was for a cause. And the cause was more money.

After the fall of Russia, during the Third World War, Maximov, with the aid of units of the Red Army loyal to him, staged a military coup. He had the other members of the Politburo killed and named himself supreme leader of the local rebel bands roaming the Russian countryside.

Within months they had organized and systematically begun taking over both Eastern and Western Europe, through cajoling, bribery, and brutality. Men like O'Malley—smiling, friendly men—kept the populace in check. People tended to pay attention to locals before they'd let their lives be swayed by foreigners.

And so it had gone, until recently.

O'Malley screwed up his James Cagney face into a portrait of a prune. Maximov had held him responsible for the last blunder. But he'd get himself out of it. He knew it.

"Stop here," O'Malley said.

"Yes, Mr. O'Malley," Mike replied. "Shall I wait in the car?"

"Of course," O'Malley said, diving from the backseat and strutting up the steps of the Clancy residence.

It was a large farm in the country, hundreds of years old. O'Malley took a deep whiff of the fresh air, remembering how bad the air had smelled in London the last time he was over there. Gunpowder. Sweat. Blood. Rebellion.

Frightening stuff.

Rancid junk.

He grabbed a huge ram's-head knocker and slammed it down on the wooden door before him four times.

Thomas Clancy, the oldest of the family, answered the door. A short, strapping man in his late forties with blazing green eyes and brown hair, Clancy led O'Malley inside.

Clancy waddled across the living room, looking like a brown-haired gnome with bad skin.

"Haven't seen you for a while," Clancy said.

"I've been preoccupied," O'Malley replied.

"So I've heard." Clancy said with a cackle.

"Whatever you've heard is exaggerated," O'Malley snapped, entering a country kitchen where a flagon of ale awaited him.

"You wouldn't be yanking my crank, now would you, Mr. O'Malley?"

"The Federated States of Europe is still in control," O'Malley said flatly. "Chairman Maximov is still in command."

"With a little bit less to command, as of four months ago." Clancy smiled.

O'Malley grimaced. He remembered what the small, elite force of Marauders had done to his official "territory," given to him by the FSE. They had executed the puppet king of England, installed a new one, and declared Britian a free and sovereign state.

Maximov had blamed O'Malley, and O'Malley found himself biding his time until he could both correct his error and destroy the Yanks.

"What happened in England was a fluke, make no mistake about that," O'Malley said.

"Still," Clancy replied, "it does shake my faith in what the FSE can do for me."

"And what you can do for the FSE?" O'Malley finished.

"Perhaps. Listen, O'Malley, before the last war, we had problems aplenty. We true Irishmen were working with the IRA, doing what we could to keep the British out. After the war things only got worse. Our town is divided in two now: the Clancys and our kind on one side, still struggling to reunite Ireland; and the Woodses on the other, still loyal to the Brits. It's madness. It grows more insane by the day."

"That's why you should continue dealing with me, Clancy." O'Malley smiled.

"With the Americans back in Europe, though—"

"What have the Americans done for you? Before the war, their government was opposed to the IRA. They sucked up to the British like a pup on its mommy's teat."

"True, but individuals came through for us, with guns and money—"

"And what have they done for you lately, eh? Nothing. *Now's* the time for you to pledge allegiance to the FSE. Your enemies will be scrambling, confused. Suddenly England isn't behind them anymore. There's a new king."

"A freedom fighter named Shatterhand," Clancy replied.

"A fool!" O'Malley said. "Nothing more. A fool who will be crushed by Chairman Maximov within months!"

"Still, the Americans—"

"There are only four Americans left." O'Malley smiled thinly. "There were only five to begin with."

"But we heard—"

"Don't trust what you hear, Mr. Clancy, trust what you *see*. Trust in your friends, your *true* friends."

Clancy massaged his brows. "Well, this might be an opportune time to strike out for reunification . . . with the Irish Republicans running around like chickens with their heads cut off."

"That's just what I was thinking." O'Malley nodded.

"So what's the story?" Clancy asked.

"A shipment of guns. A very large shipment. We hear that the black market is smuggling them in from Reykjavík, Iceland. They'll probably land up in Londonderry. We don't have the date of arrival and we don't know what the consignment is. But apparently our Icelandic friends have decided to make certain items available to King Shatterhand and the Yanks that could be put to better use by the FSE and Chairman Maximov."

Clancy frowned. "I don't know. I hate to go against the Yanks."

"Think of what you could do with ten percent of all the arms you, um, purloined?" O'Malley said. "Think of the blood that would flow from the Woodses and their supporters. Think of what it would be like to march into Belfast and blow away the British supports once and for all."

"Think of how much more blood would flow with *twenty* percent of the consignment," Clancy said with a grin.

"Twelve percent and enough cash to buy one percent more," O'Malley replied.

"It's a pleasure doing business with you, Mr. O'Malley." Clancy smiled again.

"The pleasure is all mine," O'Malley said, shaking the stocky man's hand. "And the FSE's."

O'Malley left the Clancy home and trotted to his car, where driver Mike awaited him.

"You know where to go next?"

Mike nodded. "Across town, to the Woodses' home?"

"Don't talk about, drive me there," O'Malley said.

A few minutes later O'Malley was sitting in the kitchen of William Woods, patriarch of the family and a firm supporter of the United Kingdom.

"They sullied the throne of England!" the tall, red-faced man declared, slamming his hand down on the table. He looked a tad like a beet-skinned scarecrow but with less hair. His fists were large and hard. And his blazing brown eyes shone with a hardness known only to the dead or dying.

"It's the Americans who drove them to it." O'Malley nodded sadly. "The FSE was on your side."

"Don't I know it," Woods said, simmering. "I bet the Clancys and their kind are expecting us to cave in."

"But you won't, will you?" O'Malley smiled.

"To be honest, Mr. O'Malley, with no support coming from London or the British forces, it's only a matter of time."

"Ah, but if you have arms and cash? Lots of cash?"

William Woods's eyes lit up. "I think I'm beginning to understand your visit."

"Mr. Woods," O'Malley said, "you can count on the FSE to support whatever actions you take against the so-called free Irish. You've been a loyal supporter for years. Our intelligence has learned that there's a shipment of arms arriving in Londonderry from Iceland. . . ."

Five minutes later O'Malley was in his car heading for a small seaport town where he could catch an FSE skiff to France.

One way or another, the FSE would get those arms. It didn't matter whether the pro-IRA or the pro-U.K. faction captured them for him; he'd get them all the same.

As far as he was concerned, the citizens of Northern Ireland could beat themselves silly for all eternity. All the better for the FSE. With those idiots constantly killing each other, each side would find the FSE a secret, loyal protector.

Less chance of a rebellion from either side.

Less chance for thought.

By the time anyone figured out what was going on in their country, the entire place would be a Federated base of operation; a base needed now, to take on the recently freed British.

"Pull over here, Mike," O'Malley said to his driver on a country road.

"But why, sir? We're miles from the docks."

"Mike, I pay you to drive, not to play twenty questions. Now just pull over. If you must know, we're waiting for a friend."

The two men sat in silence for a few moments.

"Roll down your window, will you, Mike?" O'Malley asked. "I'm suffocating in here."

Mike did as he was told.

"Think I'll stretch my legs," O'Malley said. He got out of the car and made a major production out of stretching his spidery hands out from his side. He bent his legs. He arched his back. He uncricked his neck.

"Winter will be here soon, Mike," O'Malley said, reaching into his topcoat.

"Yes, Mr. O'Malley, pretty soon. It's one of my favorite seasons as well."

"All's the pity that you won't be around to see it, then, Mike," O'Malley said, pulling a 9-mm from inside his coat and pointing at the surprised hulk of a driver.

O'Malley squeezed off one round.

The bullet entered just above Mike's left ear.

The force of the impact sent the body tumbling into the front passenger seat of the car. O'Malley, gun still in hand, walked up to the car and looked inside. Blood was spilling over the seat covers and onto the floor.

"Nothing personal, Mike," O'Malley said, replacing the gun with finality. "It's just that I can't let too many people know about what I do or who I see."

A large gray limousine pulled up onto the road from a clump of trees.

O'Malley smiled at the driver, an ashen-faced lad with slicked-back black hair.

The car rumbled to a halt in front of O'Malley. O'Malley swung the back door open.

"Ready for a little sea voyage?" he asked the driver.

"*Da*," the driver said.

The car bumped off along the road. Ian O'Malley headed for the sea.

Leaving a shattered, simmering country behind him.

He'd planted the seeds here, he knew.

Only time and personal ambition would bring them to fruition.

O'Malley grinned.

He had time to wait.

All the time in what was left of the world.

THREE

Buddha Chan, Freddie Mamudi, and Peter Kinski sat in King Shatterhand's private chambers at Buckingham palace. Kinski, a tall, blond, skinny, and somewhat suave Polish American with the tongue of the devil in every possible interpretation of the term, sunk low in his chair. "Has anyone seen Crazy Jack lately?"

He ran a comb through his Fabian haircut. He hated England. The hair mousse sucked.

Mamudi, wearing a Lion-faced glass eye in honor of his new adopted home base, shrugged and scratched around his zipper scar. "He's still pretty messed up. D.T.'s coupled with a concussion."

"Shit," Buddha Chan hissed. A short, squat, bald-headed man of English and Mongol ancestry who gained his name through the endless pairs of gold shooter's glasses he constantly perched on his round, slightly snubbed nose, rubbed his bald head furiously, as if for luck. "I feel sorry for Jack, you know? He's an old-fashioned sort of guy."

Mamudi nodded. "He would have been welcomed in my homeland . . . when I had a homeland," he said, referring to his Afghanistani origins. "But here? He's a fish out of water."

"A *whale* out of water," Kinski corrected.

The three men grinned.

"Do you know what this is about?" Buddha asked.

"I was hoping you did," Kinski replied.

"It is fate," Mamudi projected.

"Awww, come on, Freddie," Kinski said, wiping a slab

17

of slimy mousse from his comb. "You can just push that fate shit so far."

Mamudi smiled. "Obviously you are not spiritual."

Kinski flicked the mousse at Mamudi. "Obviously not. When I bang a girl, I don't make her part of my harem. Jeez, Mamudi. You were a lot more fun before Tom Bee died."

Mamudi shrugged. "*Life* was a lot more fun before our guru passed on to the next world."

Buddha stopped rubbing his head. "Whoops. The king is here."

King Shatterhand, a.k.a. Willis MacGregor, strode into the room.

"Shouldn't we genuflect or something?" Kinski asked.

The Marauders leapt to their feet. Kinski curtsied. Mamudi placed his two palms, as if in prayer, in front of his lips. Buddha took a deep bow.

"Sit down," Shatterhand said, waving his leather-encased fist in the air. "I'm a working policeman, not a real king, you know that."

Buddha had to take a shot. "Ah, but, Your Majesty, your subjects . . ."

Shatterhand rubbed his fiery red beard and glared at him. "My subjects are wondering why there isn't a Parliament in session and why we haven't held elections for a new prime minister and why public housing is going down the tubes and about three dozen other things I can't handle."

"Power corrupts." Kinski winked.

"And don't I know it," Shatterhand said.

He produced a file folder from beneath his good arm. "We have information from Ireland."

"Good or bad?" Buddha asked.

"Both," Shatterhand replied.

A lackey ran in with a small cardboard box and put it on Shatterhand's desk.

"What's that?" Mamudi asked.

"Later," Shatterhand replied. "This is what we have thus far. There's a shipment of arms heading our way via the Icelandic black market. Arms we need. Arms *you* need to help keep the Federated States boys in their place."

"What sort of arms?" Mamudi asked, perking up.

"We're not sure," Shatterhand said.

"They'd better be good," Kinski added, his own preference being the Russian AK-47 folding assault rifle. "Most of the stuff we've salvaged down here is at least twenty years out of date."

"I know, I know," Shatterhand admitted. "Look, I wish I could tell you more. All I know is this: The shipment is due to arrive in Londonderry in Northern Ireland. O'Malley has two families, the Clancys and the Woodses, fighting against each other in a town nearby. They're both single-minded and tunnel-visioned . . . and both FSE supporters. One is Catholic and pro-IRA, the other is Protestant and loyal to Britain. He's given *both* of the families the assignment to secure the arms, giving them a cut of the guns and the ammunition plus a wad of cash."

"How can you be sure of that?" Buddha asked.

"Because of this box," Shatterhand said with a sigh.

He opened the box slowly.

The three Marauders gasped.

Inside was a carved-up human heart.

Shatterhand looked at the heart. "The last remains of one Michael MacCrae, a man loyal to our cause, a man who hated the FSE."

"How did he—" Mamudi began.

"Nine-millimeter slug to the head," Shatterhand stated. "The carving came later."

"Who is responsible for this atrocity?" Mamudi asked.

"Don't you know?" Shatterhand grimaced.

"O'Malley," Buddha whispered. "That runty son of a—"

"You're not that tall yourself." Kinski smiled.

Buddha trained his gold-rimmed glasses on him. "I could squash him like a bug."

"If you could catch him," Shatterhand replied.

"So," Mamudi said, "what is the plan?"

"I've arranged to get you passports. Passports from Norway. Norway hasn't really been ravaged by the FSE as yet. You are to appear in Northern Ireland as traveling mercenaries. Mercenaries willing to be hired by either the Clancys or the Woodses."

"Give us a break," Kinski replied, adding hastily, "Your Highness."

"Cut it out," Shatterhand said. "Look. It's perfect. Who'd suspect a Mongol, a Pole, and a Muslim of being agents of either America or the new free Europe. Of course, you'll have to brush up on your accents. . . ."

"Anyone who knows our backgrounds will suspect," Buddha replied.

"But not very many do," Shatterhand replied. "In Ireland, you're simply known as 'foreigners,' and if you'll excuse me for saying so, you're not the traditional concept of 'foreigners,' as far as a Scot like me's concerned. So . . . ?"

"So," Kinski said, "you want us to suck up to the Clancys and the Woodses."

Buddha rubbed his round, bald head and grinned. "But in truth you want us to be hired by both."

Shatterhand laughed. "You're a wise Mongol."

"Mongols are always wise," Buddha said, removing his glasses and polishing them, revealing small, rabbitlike eyes.

Shatterhand stroked his beard. "The plan is this, my lads. Be hired by both. Let both sides, both families, think that you're working for them and spying on the other clan. Keep them on edge. And then, when one of them makes a move for the weaponry. . ."

"We nab them." Kinski sighed, again producing his comb and sending it sliding through his hair. "Yeah, yeah, yeah. No big deal. One question, though: What about Crazy Jack Keenan?"

Shatterhand suddenly became very, very regal. "I'm afraid there's no question there."

"What do you mean?" zipper-faced Mamudi asked.

"He assaulted a police officer," Shatterhand replied.

"Twenty-six, I believe," Buddha added, glaring at Shatterhand from beneath his shades. "And let's face it, most of your police are green-faced wusses . . . as, may I add, are most of your armed forces."

"That's beside the point," Shatterhand answered. "He's been given as much leeway as I can possibly provide. The man has to go to court and be sentenced as any common criminal. I'm sorry."

"So are we," Kinski said. "Because we're not going without him."

"What?" Shatterhand thundered.

"Calm down, Your Highness," Buddha replied. "Jack is part of our team. We're not lifting a thumb . . ."

"Finger," Kinski injected.

Buddha went on, ". . . until he's out of, what's the word for it, *stir*?"

Now it was Mamudi's turn. "Jack is a very troubled, very spiritual man, Shatterhand. A man as spiritual as the late Tom Bee. You remember Thomas, don't you, sir? The American Indian who gave his life to save your people? In his own way Jack is akin to Bee.

"He believes in worlds we have never seen. He mourns for a life long gone. In many religions he would be revered as a teacher, a spiritual leader of the human race. He holds pain within him that not you, or any of us, will ever know. He has a powerful mind, Your Highness, which makes his pain greater. He *is* a religious man, whether he cops to it or not.

"You look at one, definitive world, and he sees many, running through infinity at the same time. Yet he chooses to stay in *our* world and do the best he can to elevate it to a greater plane. He is a fighter. He is a man with a great soul. We have all seen evidence of that. And if you don't include him on this mission, then, by all the gods, I must say to you, stick it up your ass."

"But your president sent you," Shatterhand growled.

"Our president is miles away." Kinski shrugged.

Buddha grinned. "We could be outa here, with five dozen bobbies dead, before you could ever contact the president."

"But that's mutiny!" Shatterhand thundered.

"Nope," Kinski said, giggling. "That's *smarts*."

"Either get Jack out . . . ," Buddha added.

"Or save your fucking world for yourself," Kinski concluded.

"Pardon his euphemism." Mamudi grinned.

He plucked out his glass eye. "You don't mind if I polish my *good* eye while you make the call?"

Shatterhand simmered. "I knew you all were a rowdy bunch."

"We managed to save your country's ass," Buddha said. "Don't ever forget it. And if you want us to go in and slice Ireland off the FSE's pick-hits list . . ."

"You'd better dial Scotland Yard," Mamudi continued.

Mamudi fished into his vest pocket. "If you don't have the number, I'm sure I have it somewhere here for you."

Shatterhand stared at the three men. His gaze passed from face to face.

Suddenly, without warning, he reared back into his chair and emitted a loud, roaring laugh.

"Goddamn," he howled, "you four should always be with me. Promise me . . . if I ever start taking myself too seriously again, you'll be around to bite my butt."

"Promise." Kinski grinned.

"I have the molars for it." Buddha chortled.

"And I will pray for the remnants of your heroic soul," Mamudi said, "if fate allows."

Shatterhand stared at them all. "Bastards."

"Only one of us." Kinski smiled. "But you have to guess who."

"You don't have to give me the number. I know it," Shatterhand said.

He picked up the phone and dialed. "Hello? Inspector Munru? This is King Shatterhand. Yes. Yes. Thank you. You don't have to say that. Now listen. There's a man who has just been let out of hospital and admitted back into the prison. Yes, Captain Jack. I know his head is a mess. Always has been, as far as I can tell. I want you to let him go. I'll send a car for him later."

Shatterhand glanced at the three Marauders in front of him.

"And officially, Inspector, never, *ever*, take him into police custody again. The man is an agent working for his king. Whatever he does, it's for a reason. Is that understood? Yes, yes, thank you."

Shatterhand faced the three Marauders. "Satisfied?"

Buddha, Kinski, and Mamudi nodded. "Thank you, Your Highness."

"Oh, can it," Shatterhand said.

"Any other business?" Kinski asked.

"Gentlemen," Buddha said, "I believe a round of high-fives are in order."

The four men slapped palms and the three Marauders left their king.

Shatterhand stood behind his desk for a moment. He watched the door close.

"Gentlemen," he whispered, "I hope God will be with you. If he isn't . . . the devil will be biting at your heels."

He slouched down behind his desk, wishing he were still a small-town Scot cop with a family, and a future, and a land that wasn't poisoned by both radiation and the Federated States of Europe.

He wished the past had never happened.

When he was done with that, he gnashed his teeth, pounded his desk, and vowed to forge a better, freer future.

He winced.

He looked down at his hand. Splinters. They didn't make desks like they did before the last war.

He began picking the splinters from his hand.

One by one.

By one.

In the back of his mind he envisioned the globe as being "normal" again.

In front of his mind he saw enslavement, brutality, and slow-slinking postnuclear disease.

He smiled to himself.

And he wished for magic.

He wished for the world he had always wanted for his butchered family.

FOUR

Crazy Jack Keenan awoke with a start. Someone was opening his jail cell. He blinked his eyes, rubbed them, and recognized the faces of Buddha, Kinski, Mamudi, and Shatterhand.

"Is this a jailbreak?" he muttered, scratching his aching skull.

"Consider it a reprieve," Shatterhand muttered, "and if it were up to me, you wouldn't get it."

"I take it, then, that the decision isn't yours," Crazy Jack said, getting to his feet.

"We're off to Ireland," Kinski said.

"Ah, the Emerald Isle," Jack replied. "Never been there. Always wanted to go."

"It's not intended to be a vacation," Shatterhand spat.

"Didn't think so," Jack replied, walking out of the cell. "What are we up against?"

"The usual." Mamudi smirked. "Us against them."

"How many of them?" Jack asked.

"Just about everybody," Buddha responded.

"Those are my kind of odds." Jack smiled. "Fill me in on the way over. By the way, how *are* we getting over there?"

"Fishing boat to Londonderry," Kinski said.

"Good. I'm famished," Jack said.

"Aw, Jack," Buddha said.

"Hey, I used to like sushi," Jack said.

"Once you get there, you're on your own," Shatterhand said.

"What a surprise," Jack muttered. He stared at the king. "Now, if you'll get out of my way, I'll go back to my apartment, wash up, and get the hell out of this veddy proper city. And if you don't get out of my way, I will fulfill my desire to crack the jaw of someone who's considered royalty."

Shatterhand chuckled. "You *are* an American, aren't you?"

Jack found himself grinning. "That's what I've been trying to let you know since you put my keester on ice two months ago."

Shatterhand smiled and stepped aside. The three other Marauders shrugged and followed Jack out of the prison.

"We're going to need winter clothes, parkas," Jack said. "Londonderry is in Northern Ireland. My guess is that little Irish jerk-off O'Malley is involved in this and we're trying to bust something up. They'll probably be sending us in as mercs from the north. We'll have to dress and act the part. I'll be the only Yank, I suppose. You three will trade in on your heritage. We'll have to be heavily armed and macho our way through it. If we don't, we're dead meat."

The three other Marauders, following Jack, glanced at each other.

"How does he do that?" Buddha asked.

"He's spiritual," Mamudi said.

"If you consider spirits coming from a bottle," Kinski agreed, "I'll buy that."

The three men followed Jack out of Scotland Yard and entered a government car. They rode into the darkness together.

The North Sea is never very friendly, and with winter just around the corner, it snaps at all intruders like a hungry serpent.

Aboard the small fishing boat, the four Marauders found themselves bobbing and tilting above the whitecapped waves of the storm-tossed sea. Only Mamudi, the former SEAL, was enjoying it.

"Isn't the ocean wonderful?" he asked.

"If you like barfing into it," Jack replied. "Do we have a vehicle waiting for us when we get there?"

"Affirmative," Buddha replied.

"Backup?" Jack asked.

"*Nada*," Kinski answered. "Not a soul."

"Great." Jack groaned. "Another well-planned suicide maneuver. All right, then we better start fabricating our pasts—and fast. We're mercs and we've been traveling around the north for quite a while. Who's the best at geography?"

The three other Marauders stared at each other sheepishly.

"I suppose *I* am," Buddha replied. "Why?"

"Go inside and figure out a half dozen cities we might have 'liberated' in one way or another. Just write down a laundry list. Give me the cities and the populations and what weaponry we'd use. I'll bullshit. . . ."

He turned to Kinski. "No, actually, I think Silver Tongue should bullshit anybody who asks too many questions. Remember, once we get there, we have no first names, no ranks, no pasts. We're just four men. A unit. That's all anybody has to know. The more mysterious we are, the better the locals will like it."

Jack left the deck of the ship, Buddha following.

Kinski turned to Mamudi. "I've never seen him like this."

Mamudi smiled. "He has the soul of a warrior. A warrior lives for battle. For a warrior there is nothing more valuable than victory, except for honor. Jack is an honorable man."

"But they call him Crazy!"

"Isn't it crazy to attempt honor in today's world?" Mamudi said, walking off the deck.

Kinski stared at the storm-tossed sea ahead of him. "What a fucking world we live in."

Mamudi tensed. "Get Jack."

"Why?"

Mamudi focused his good eye on the sea. "Trouble. Three men in a lightweight boat. Heavily armed."

"How can you be sure of that?"

"I have eyes, uh, an *eye*, don't I?"

Within seconds Jack was back on deck. "What do we have?"

"Three of the most unlikely fishermen I've ever seen," Mamudi said. "Speedboat. Motor cut."

Jack glanced at Kinski. "Tell the captain to cut the engines. Tell him we're going to stare at the night sky for . . . a half hour or so."

Jack looked at Mamudi. Freddie was already stripping out of his parka and clothing. He had a wet suit on underneath. "Should be okay."

"Are you *sure* they're FSE men?" Jack asked.

"Call it intuition," Mamudi said, twisting his thin face into that of an eager boy.

"I call it damned dangerous," Jack said. "The water's cold."

"I'll survive," Mamudi said.

"You can't use explosives to take them out," Jack reminded him. "In case there are other goons around."

Mamudi reached into his utility belt, producing a British-issue Fairbairn-Sykes commando knife. "This should do it," he said.

Jack handed him a flare pistol. "If you need backup, use this."

"I won't need it," Mamudi said. "But thanks."

"Freddie . . . ," Jack began.

"You don't have to tell me." Mamudi grinned. "If I don't succeed, the entire mission could be scrubbed. And if I don't succeed, then there'll be only *three* Marauders."

Jack wrapped his massive hand around Mamudi's thin right shoulder. "It's the latter I was thinking of, you heathen."

"I know *that*." Freddie grinned, diving into the sea.

Jack peered into the angry gloom.

He could barely make out the speedboat.

Aboard the small craft, three Eastern European sentries sat alert. They had been told to watch for a shipment of arms. To alert the area's FSE operative, O'Malley, as soon as the cargo vessel was in sight.

So far there was nothing in the vicinity but a chugging fishing trawler.

One of the men glanced at his watch. In another thirty minutes he'd check in with O'Malley to let him know their status. Tomorrow there would be a backup unit in place on the Londonderry docks. That would make things easier.

The guard stared at the fishing boat.

Why had it stopped?

He began to tense up.

He motioned to his two companions.

All instinctively picked up their Daewoo AR100 assault rifles. At six and a half pounds each and thirty-eight inches in length, they were handy little devils when it came to skirmishes.

All three men gazed at the fishing boat.

As they did so, a merman suddenly appeared from behind them.

The first guard caught the movement in the water. He yelled something in Czech. Roughly translated, it amounted to "a creature from the sea is attacking!"

The three men whirled.

By that time Mamudi, knife drawn, was already in action. A trained SEAL, he locked his mind into "offense" mode.

Moving like an Atlantan samurai, he slithered across the boat. He decapitated the first guard, disemboweled the second, and split the third guard's head down to his shoulders.

When he was sure all three FSE sentries were no longer a threat, he moved to the forward section of the boat and turned the engine over. He aimed the boat toward the distant horizon and then dived overboard into the icy sea.

On the fishing trawler, Jack watched the speedboat pick up speed as it aimlessly headed out on the route to oblivion.

He took a deep breath of cold, foggy air.

Then he spotted something heading toward the trawler, something swimming with the ease of an otter.

It was Mamudi.

Jack lowered a rope ladder for the exhausted SEAL.

Mamudi slowly climbed up the ladder.

"You were right about the water," he said, wheezing. "It's colder than a witch's tit."

Jack wrapped a towel around the skinny Marauder. "What about the men in the boat?"

"As of now," Freddie said, teeth chattering, "they are headed for their rightful place with either God or the fellow with the pitchfork."

"No problems?"

Mamudi shrugged. "It depends on where they choose to spend their afterlife, doesn't it?"

FIVE

The four men clad in pale gray parkas clung to the jeep as Crazy Jack, consulting a map, maneuvered it toward the small town of Feirgall. They passed a lighthouse. It wasn't battered. It wasn't in a state of disrepair. Yet it was dark.

Deserted.

The waves of the open sea crashed harmlessly off its rocky, barren base.

"Not a good sign," Jack surmised.

"Why's that?" Kinski asked. "They could have just shut it off."

"Why?" Jack asked.

"They might not want to attract attention," Buddha answered.

"This is FSE territory," Jack replied. "They have no one to be afraid of. They know the British haven't got the strength to take them on conventionally, and the only Americans in the area amount to a smattering. So why douse the beacon?"

"Okay, okay, Mr. Green Beret." Kinski sighed, exasperated. "Why is it out?"

"Beats me," Jack replied. "Maybe it's a result of a feud."

"The Clancys and the Woodses?" Mamudi replied. "How would that affect sea traffic?"

"You of all people should know that God works in mysterious ways," Jack said with a cackle.

Mamudi laughed in response, desperately clutching the two trunks of armaments the Marauders had tossed into the back of the jeep. Jack was not the best of drivers in normal

31

circumstances. And, unfortunately, Mamudi had never known Jack in any circumstance that could even remotely be considered normal.

"Look! Up ahead!" Kinski said.

Jack slowed the jeep down. On the outskirts of the small coastal village stood two small cottages. They must have been three hundred years old, easily. Made of stucco and brick. Thatched roofs. Large oak beams supporting the exteriors. Something straight out of Shakespeare country.

Yet they had been improved upon.

The cottage to the left of the jeep boasted barred windows and doors, the kind seen in New York and the ghetto neighborhoods of every major city in America before the nuke-out. But here? In the middle of nowheresville?

"That doesn't make sense," Mamudi said.

An old woman was banging on the wooden door of the cottage to the left of the jeep. Three large Irishmen emerged, sawed-off shotguns in their hands.

"Get away from here, you," the first man roared. "We've warned you!" He pounded his chest as if he were the short, stout first cousin of King Kong.

"But I must see her!" the old lady cried.

"Well, you *won't*," the man replied.

He raised his sawed-off shotgun. "Now, you have ten seconds to get back into your hovel or we'll blow out your scheming Papist gizzards."

The woman backed away.

The fat man began to count. "Ten, nine, eight . . . I'm warning you, traitor . . . six, five . . ."

"That doesn't seem like a fair fight to me," Jack said, pressing the pedal to the metal of the jeep and sending it screaming to a halt directly between the quivering old lady and the fat man.

The fat man and his two minions looked up with a start, raising their sawed-off shotguns toward Jack.

Jack noticed a beautiful young blond woman gazing mournfully from the window of the cottage behind the three goons. She spotted Jack and turned from the window.

Jack faced the trio.

"Excuse me, lads," he said, affecting his best nondenominational U.K. accent. "Could you direct me to Feirgall?"

The fat man stepped before the jeep, exposing his sallow, pockmarked mug to the harsh headlights. "Who wants to know?"

"And who's that who's asking?" Jack grinned.

The two other men brought their shotguns up.

Kinski raised his AK-47 at the two men, trying to remember his Polish origins. "Uh-uh, boys. Before you even squeeze the trigger, you'll be late."

The two men lowered their guns.

The fat man in front of the jeep hesitated.

The old lady ran into her barred cottage and slammed the door.

"At least *she's* safe," Buddha hissed.

Jack glared at the man in the headlights. "We're not looking for a fight, boyo." He smiled. "Just employment."

The fat man considered this. "Well, we're always looking for new men."

"We?" Mamudi smiled.

"*Us,*" the fat man repeated.

"Oh, *us,*" Mamudi replied.

Jack wasn't impressed. "Well, *someone* will find four at the nearest hotel in town." He smiled.

"Three miles straight ahead," the fat man, named Mac-Millan said. "There's only one hotel in the city. Barney's."

"I'll look for it." Jack grinned and gunned the gas, causing the fat man to jump out of the way.

"Nice little mess we're getting into," Jack said.

"You could have just jeopardized our whole mission," Kinski said, lowering his gun and producing a comb. He ran it through his hair while he sat in the backseat.

"If I honestly thought that," Jack said, "I would have taken all three of the pasty-faced assholes out."

Mamudi smiled silently as the jeep rumbled through the night.

Behind them, MacMillan glared at the jeep.

He turned to one of his pale-faced lackeys. "Call Woods. Tell him there's trouble coming to town. Tell him that I personally want to see them all dead."

"Yes, sir," one of the two boys said as he nodded and lumbered back into the cottage.

In the jeep, Jack sat behind the wheel and thought of the girl with the golden hair, seemingly imprisoned in the small home.

Why was she there?

Why was the old woman trying so desperately to gain entrance?

Why couldn't Jack get her out of his mind?

He drove on toward the town, letting his mind drift.

He remembered a barbecue.

His wife beside him.

His buddies from the Green Berets had brought their families as well.

They had played games that day.

The men had tossed horseshoes, and then they'd watched a baseball doubleheader on the tube.

The wives had gone through a few hands of poker before leading the kids into the shoddy plastic pool in the concrete backyard. A plastic pool was all Jack could afford on military pay.

He remembered turning from the tube and walking to the window. His eyes trained themselves on his wife.

She had looked positively beatific that day.

So *young,* so *alive.*

And the children . . . God, how the children shimmered in the sunlight, frolicking in the pool.

Dead now.

All dead.

So young, so full of life, obliterated so swiftly.

Jack clutched the wheel.

If he could save one . . . just *one.*

SIX

The jeep, containing the four Marauders, rumbled into the town of Feirgall. It wasn't so much a conventional town as a slice out of history—a village, really. Thatched-roof cottages lined the side streets. The tiny main street of town housed the shops, the inn, and one or two small pubs.

Buddha Chan rubbed his shaved head nervously as the jeep sputtered down the deserted street.

"Not much of a welcoming committee." Jack grimaced, scanning the small street for any sign of activity. "And by this time, *you* know *they* know we're coming."

"Does the term *sitting duck* mean anything to you?" Kinski said, riding shotgun.

"There's Barney's up ahead," Mamudi said, squinting his good eye.

In the middle of the street was a dilapidated inn, an old structure that had been added to over the years. Now it resembled a gingerbread cottage with two small shoeboxes affixed to its side.

"Slow it down, Jack," Buddha said, the drab fall sun reflecting off his polished glasses. "I smell something funny."

"It's probably Kinski's hair spray," Jack said, easing his foot off the accelerator.

Mamudi, in the back of the jeep with Buddha Chan, placed a hand on Kinski's shoulder.

"Flanking us," he whispered.

Kinski nodded. He had already spotted the movement. On either side of the street were two mercs. One, a large fellow armed with a Unique F-11 .22 long rifle, a semiautomatic carbine of the bullpup design, crouched behind a half-opened wood-and-glass door. He was to the left of the jeep.

Another thug perched on a rooftop, huddling close to its sloped design. He wielded the Armi Jager .22 rimfire AP-80, basically an Italian version of the AK-47.

Two more assholes hovered in the shadows, Intratech Scorpion assault pistols in their hands. Shoddy stuff. Not made for *real* fighting.

Kinski sighed. Obviously these local mercenaries had never seen real combat.

It was one thing to shoot down a priest, a minister, or a half-drunk local. It was another thing to take on real fighting men. "Tsk, tsk," he said over his shoulder. "You want the left or the right?"

Mamudi grinned. "Left."

Jack slowed the jeep down even more. "Whenever you're ready, gentlemen. I'd appreciate not getting my goddamn head blown off before we get to unpack."

Mamudi and Kinski took deep breaths and, exhaling suddenly, swung their bodies around in rapid, almost feline motion.

Mamudi reached down into a small satchel of knives and produced a heavy bowie model. Buddha Chan slithered down into the backseat as Mamudi casually sent the knife spiraling, slicing through the air.

The knife, its blade smashing through the glass of the door, found its mark.

A choked scream emerged from behind the door. It slammed shut, inward. Within seconds a pool of blood formed under the door, spreading onto the sidewalk.

"A bleeding door," Jack muttered. "I'd say that qualifies as a miracle in *any* religion."

The man on the roof scrambled to action. He raised his weapon, and by the time he had, Kinski had lifted his treasured AK-47 and fired a powerful burst at the would-be assassin. The man didn't have the presence of mind either to seek cover or screech.

He took the slugs across his chest, a dumbfounded look playing across his face.

The Marauders watched the pea-brained sniper tumble down the side slope of the roof and make his ungraceful exit into a nearby alley.

Kinski sent a casual spray of lead across the two men in the shadows.

The two fools had never realized the chance to raise their Scorpions.

By the time they had figured it all out, their brains were dribbling down onto their shoulders.

Tough break.

Jack shook his head sadly. He glanced in the rearview mirror at Buddha. "Feeling less nervous, now, Chan?"

Buddha Chan smiled thinly. "It's not over yet, Jack."

"Hope not," Jack said, angling the jeep up to the curbside before Barney's. "We're just beginning to make an impression on this town."

The four Marauders leapt out of the jeep and entered the dark, publike atmosphere of Barney's.

They were greeted by a half dozen stone-faced men. "Howya doin'?" Jack nodded, leading his three comrades to a small table. A barmaid, who looked a tad like a vulture, hovered above them.

"What'll it be?" she asked.

"Four lagers," Jack said with a smile. "And we'll be needing rooms for a while."

The woman tossed a nervous glance at the small, fidgeting man behind the bar. He shook his head no.

"I'm afraid we're all booked up," the woman muttered.

Jack produced a fistful of five-pound notes. "You still accept this as money, don't you?"

The woman gaped at the newfound riches thrust before her. "Aye, we do."

"And I don't think we've arrived at the peak of tourist season. Do you?"

The woman tilted her head toward the money and glanced at the owner, behind the bar.

He shrugged.

"Well," she said, "I suppose we could vacate a few rooms for you."

"I'd appreciate it." Jack grinned, flashing a sly smile while rubbing his left hand through his mass of orange locks. "Now, maybe, along with those lagers, we'd like some bangers and mash."

"Yes, sir," the woman said, scurrying back toward the manager.

"Think we've established our presence enough?" Jack winked at his friends.

"Probably too much," Buddha replied. "While you wait for your grub, I think I'll take a quick whizz, if you know what I mean."

Mamudi grinned at the short, rotund man. "You're a genius, Buddha."

Buddha Chan's eyes crinkled behind his shooter's glasses as he smiled. "No. Just realistic."

The round man waddled off as Crazy Jack, Freddie Mamudi, and Kinski sat, awaiting their brew.

Before long, a long, thin young man stormed into the pub. His face was studded with red splotches and his hair was blond and wild. He marched up to the three men, holding something behind his back.

"I believe you *lost* this," he hissed, tossing Mamudi's bowie knife onto the Marauders' tabletop.

Mamudi eyed the knife. "You know, I was wondering where I dropped this. You are so kind. May the gods smile upon you."

"You killed two of my men," the young gunman announced, whipping out a Holmes MP-83 from his long trench coat. He trained the 9-mm parabellum assault pistol at the three Marauders.

Jack wasn't impressed. "Want a lager?" he asked. "Or would you prefer ale?"

The skinny young man gaped at him, fuming. "This isn't a joke, mister."

Jack nodded. "It *is* a joke. Those four assholes who tried to kill us were about as subtle as circus elephants. Never confuse hayseeds with guns with gunmen, sonny."

The young man grew red. "And who the hell do you think you are?"

"Just your run-of-the-mill mercs"—Mamudi shrugged —"trying to make a living."

"Just trying to get by," Kinski added. "You'll excuse me if I comb my hair? Your climate doesn't do a lot for the front wave."

Kinski whipped out a comb and began fondling his long locks. The kid was stymied.

"Who do you work for?" he demanded.

"Whoever'll hire us," Jack replied.

"You a Yank?" the young man asked.

"Once upon a time," Jack said, shrugging his massive shoulders. "And Kinski here was a Ukie, and Mamudi was a Sunni."

"I'm still a Sunni," Mamudi corrected.

The young man blinked, not comprehending a word.

"Sunni Muslim," Mamudi said with a wink of his good eye. "Check your history books. It's full of folks like me. Try Persia."

"It's been called Iran for years," Kinski said.

"Old habits die hard," Mamudi replied.

The young man was thoroughly confused now. He trained his weapon on the three men. "Well," he said. "My father, William Woods, could probably use some trained men, although he's not going to be happy about the four soldiers you killed."

"They weren't soldiers," Jack reminded him. "*We're* soldiers. *They* were assholes."

The young man clenched his teeth. "Come with me," he ordered.

Jack glanced at his two comrades. "Naaah."

"What?" the young man said. "I'm Willy Woods! My father *runs* half of this town!"

"Well"—Jack smiled—"maybe we're sitting in the wrong half. Look here, sonny."

"Willy!" the young man blustered.

"Willy, then. If your daddy wants to hire us, let him get his butt down here and talk to us in person. We don't deal with kids."

"I'm nineteen!" Willy declared.

"My socks are older than you are. Now go tell Papa that if he's looking for four good men, he can find us at Barney's."

Willy glowered, raising his weapon. "I could kill you all right now." He grinned, his crooked teeth emerging from behind chapped lips.

"Willy, Willy, Willy." Kinski sighed. "Listen carefully. Jack just said your papa could hire *four* good men. Now, how many do you see sitting here at this table?"

Willy, relying on his public-school math, quickly calculated that there were only three men at the table.

He heard a click from behind him. "Drop the peashooter, sonny" came the voice of Buddha Chan.

Willy gulped and did as he was told.

Buddha walked up to the boy, his pudgy right hand carrying a Colt government-model Mark IV .45-caliber automatic pistol.

Buddha put a reassuring arm around the young kid's shoulder. "Now, the thing is, my friend, we are four friends who don't care *who* we work for. Anyone who pays us well, we'll defend. But we don't ever, *ever* work for dopes."

Willy was confused now.

Buddha Chan smiled and pushed his shades up to his eyes. "Let me show you what I mean. You come in with that piece-of-crap toy, train it on my buddies, and expect them to grovel, right? Well, it doesn't work that way. We're a team, you see. And we're very, very experienced when it comes to dealing with weekend warriors. I'll give you a quick demonstration."

He turned to the barmaid. "May we have a fork, miss?"

The woman nodded nervously and trotted to the table, dropping a fork on the tabletop before scurrying away. Buddha Chan smiled at the young country lad. "Now pick up the fork."

The boy did as he was told.

Buddha nodded. "Good lad. Now toss the fork as high as you can toward the ceiling."

The boy gulped and sent the fork flying.

Buddha whipped out his .45 and, squinting his rabbit eyes behind his shades, squeezed off four quick rounds.

The fork zigged and zagged high above their heads, Buddha sending four .45-caliber bullets into its silver frame.

From above the fork, pieces of the plaster ceiling began to shower down onto the tabletops.

Buddha lowered his hand.

The badly mutilated fork fell onto the floor of Barney's. The men in the bar remained totally silent.

Buddha, his arm still around Willy Woods, hugged him closer, raising the .45 to the boy's nose. "Now," he said, chuckling, "the next time you *ever* think of raising a weapon in my friends' direction, know, in your heart of hearts, that I will create a third nostril in your breezer here. I'm a Mongol. Taras Bulba was a Mongol. He was not— repeat, *not*—a nice man to cross. Do you understand that, son?"

Willy was sweating now. He nodded his head up and down in the herky-jerky motion of a marionette sans strings.

"I'm glad we understand each other," Buddha said, re-holstering his gun and sliding into his chair. "Now, if you'll excuse us, we're hungry and thirsty. We've traveled a long way to get here."

Jack smiled up at the boy. "Now, if your daddy wants to come and talk to us, he's welcome."

Willy backed toward the door of the pub.

"And by the way," Mamudi said. "If you're thinking about any of your hayseeds trying to rob our jeep—"

A scream cut the air from outside.

Mamudi sighed. "It's booby-trapped."

A fat young man staggered into the room, a butterfly knife through his neck.

Mamudi shook his head sadly and walked over to the dead young idiot. He removed the knife. He smiled at the shaken Willy Woods. "Tripwire," he said with a shrug. "You can't beat them."

Willy Woods skittered out of the pub.

Mamudi sat himself back at the table as the barmaid

trotted over with the men's bangers and mash, beef sausage and mashed potatoes.

"I'll pay for the damage to the ceiling." Buddha Chan grinned at her.

"Thank you sir, that's very kind," she blurted before scurrying off.

"I'll be sure to tell Barney," she added over her shoulder.

"Nice shooting." Jack nodded toward Buddha.

Buddha shoved a forkful of mashed potatoes toward his face. "Of course." He grinned before opening wide.

SEVEN

The Marauders had just finished eating when a short, squat man ambled over toward them from the bar. He had brown hair and gleaming green eyes.

"You're mercenaries, are ya?" he asked.

Jack shrugged. "We like to think of ourselves as technical advisers."

The man emitted a wide smile. "Then you're probably just the kind of men I can use."

"And who," Mamudi said, leaning back in his chair, "are *you*?"

The barrel-chested man stuck his hands in his pockets. "Thomas Clancy is the name. A local lad from way back. Right now I'm interested in fighting back the Protestant hordes from my homeland."

"You're a Catholic, then?" Mamudi asked.

"Indeed I am," Clancy said proudly.

"Don't go talking about religion to me," Kinski said, while you have that gun tucked behind your belt."

Clancy laughed. Indeed he had a Colt tucked in the back of his pants, just above the spine. "You have good eyes, Russkie."

"Okie," Kinski corrected. "Or maybe Polack. Jeez. It's all the same these days, I guess."

Clancy rubbed a callused left hand across his stubbly chin. "Would you like to have dinner at my place?"

Buddha peered at the man from behind his glasses. "We still have to unpack."

"I'll send a driver," Clancy said. "My brother, Ryan.

You won't be able to miss him. He has hair as red as this Titan over here, and a big, silver crucifix 'round his neck."

"Give us an hour?" Jack asked.

"You've got it, Yank." Clancy nodded before striding out of the inn.

"Looks like we're *in*," Kinski said.

"We'll see," Crazy Jack replied.

Two hours later the Marauders found themselves seated around Thomas Clancy's massive dining table, eating roast duck. Surrounding Clancy were his brothers; Ryan and Sean, and his sons, Tommy and Jack.

He addressed the Marauders midway through the dinner. "Gentlemen, you may not know it, but you've done us a great service today."

"How so?" Jack asked.

Clancy grinned. "Why, you took out three of Woods's men."

"And who, may I ask, is Woods?" Mamudi winked.

"He's the devil himself," Clancy replied. "You may not be familiar with these parts, but for quite some time we've been beset by the Troubles!"

"The Troubles?" Buddha Chan repeated.

"Aye." Clancy nodded. "You see, once upon a time there was an Ireland, and then the Brits moved in, severing the country in two. The south, the *real* Ireland, is *truly* Irish. Roman Catholic. Independent. A sovereign state. But the north? Ah, that's another story. We were beaten into submission, we were. The British took over and forced the Church of England down our throats. The Orangemen took over and beat the true Greenmen into the dust. But we haven't given up, boys. We've just begun to fight."

"So," Jack replied, "what you want us to do is take up a religious war?"

"No, my son," Clancy replied. "We want you to join us in *freeing* Ireland from the corrupt United Kingdom!"

"I thought Britain had just gone through a revolution itself," Kinski offered.

"I don't *trust* it," Clancy replied.

"Why?" Buddha asked.

"The Brits have always been after our asses." Clancy nodded sagely. "And that's a fact."

"How does the FSE figure into all of this?" Mamudi asked.

"Well," Clancy said with a wink, "between you and I, the FSE is supporting the Catholics up here. They *want* a United Ireland."

"And why is that?" Jack asked.

"Well, suppose you were one of the FSE men?" Clancy suggested. "Wouldn't you rather have one *united* country behind you, as opposed to a fragmented nation?"

"And you support the FSE?" Buddha replied.

Clancy shrugged. "I support anybody who will drive the British from our soil."

"And suppose the FSE has gone and sided with Woods?" Kinski asked.

"They wouldn't *think* of it." Clancy grinned. "The Woods clan represents *all* that has kept Ireland halved for the last century. It's in the FSE's interest to *unite* the nation, I tell you!"

The Marauders lapsed into silence. "So," Jack broached, "how do we fit in?"

"Well," Clancy said, leaning over the table, "in order to reunite Ireland, we need artillery—guns, ammunition. And cunning. I have been told that there's a shipment of pretty heavy-duty weaponry arriving hereabouts, and soon. If we can garner those guns before the scum-sucking Orangemen have the smarts to smell them out, we have a good chance of liberating these parts from the Brit lovers. We'll then be able to march into Ulster and make the other side see the error of their way."

"And you want *us* to help you secure the weaponry?" Mamudi asked.

"Sure as hell I do," Clancy said. "I saw how you handled Woods's men today. His men have held this town in check since the last war. Even before then. You treated them as if they were choirboys."

Buddha Chan rubbed his head. "They seemed pretty green to me." He smiled. "No pun intended."

"Maybe so," Clancy replied. "But they have managed to

outgun us, man for man, for the last decade."

"How much is this worth to you?" Jack asked.

Clancy thought hard. "Fifty thousand pounds," he offered. "Plus ten percent of any booty we garner while marching south."

"Twenty percent," Mamudi countered.

"Fifteen," Clancy stated. "Say, you aren't Jewish, are you?"

"Muslim." Mamudi winked.

"Aren't you all from the same area?" Clancy asked.

"We have our differences," Mamudi replied graciously.

"All right," Clancy said. "Fifteen."

"Now that *that's* all settled," Jack replied, "what would you like us to do?"

"Ideally, I would like you to go back to Barney's and make out that you've refused my offer. Side with the Woodses. If at all possible, spy on them, and then report back to me."

"Double agents, so to speak," Kinski said.

"Aye." Clancy grinned. "Isn't that a beauty of an idea?"

"It is," Jack said. "But we'll need two things from you."

"And what might those be?"

"First we have to have your assurance that nobody, and I mean *nobody,* not even your closest relations, know that we're spying for you."

"Agreed."

"Second of all," Jack said, smiling, "we'll need some cash up front."

"I'll give you half," Clancy said.

"You have yourself a deal," Buddha answered. "How well-stocked are you in terms of ammunition?"

"We could use more," Clancy admitted.

"We're running low," Kinski replied.

"Whatever we have, you are welcome to it," Clancy said, rising and extending a hand.

The four Marauders shook his hand in turn. "You have yourself four new men, Mr. Clancy." Crazy Jack grinned.

"I knew I could count on a man with red hair," Clancy said.

"One small question," Jack began.

"I thought I'd made myself clear," Clancy replied.

"It hasn't anything to do with our plan," Jack said. "On our way into town, far on the outskirts, we passed two small cottages near a lighthouse."

Clancy's face grew grim. "Hell itself."

"We saw a young girl, imprisoned by fully armed men in one cottage," Jack continued. "And an old woman in the one across the street."

"That's just a touch of what the Woodses will do," Clancy said.

"Molly," Clancy said with a moan. "Molly McGuire is the young woman's name. She's the daughter of Henry and Agnes McGuire. Henry was the lighthouse keeper until recently."

"Was?" Jack asked.

"You see," Clancy continued, "after the last war there was a general upheaval, as you can imagine. The McGuires were fine, outstanding citizens of the area. Catholic, they were. True Irishmen. Then the Woodses began to think that they could just kind of *take over* everything. They figured that with people's minds occupied, nobody would notice if they flexed their muscles a bit.

"Willy Woods had his eye on young Molly, but she'd have none of him. Well, feeling his oats, he went out one fine day and decided to take her."

"Take her?" Buddha Chan asked.

"You know," Clancy replied, "snatch her. Well, Molly's father would have none of that. The Woods clan was known to be Orangemen. He defended her honor, he did."

"And died for it," Kinski rejoined.

"That he did." Clancy nodded. "Double-barreled shotgun through the chest. He suffered."

"And Molly?" Jack asked.

"Snatched," Clancy grimaced. "Imprisoned. Young Willy Woods takes her from her prison every weekend to do with her as he pleases at the Woods home."

"And her mother?" Buddha asked.

Clancy frowned. "Her mother? Well, she was allowed to live in her old home, directly across from Molly's prison.

It was, at the time, deemed to be a mercy, but in fact, it's a slow, lingering torture.

"Every day she tries to make her way to her daughter, and every day she is forced away. She sits there, like a tossed-off guardian angel, just waiting for the chance to free her poor daughter. It's a sad state, it is."

Jack nodded. "It seemed so to me."

"Molly's a lost cause, I'm afraid," Clancy stated.

"Not necessarily," Jack answered.

"Don't go diddling in things that don't matter," Clancy advised.

"Don't tell me what matters and what doesn't," Jack said. "You'd be surprised about what falls into place in the scheme of things. I had a wife and a son. They were considered civilians. Unimportant in the military sense of the word. One of the world's 'acceptable losses.' Yet, it's because of them that I'm here."

"What happened to them?" Clancy asked.

"I don't fuggin' know," Jack replied. "And as of now, that lack of knowledge pushes me onward. That is what brings me to you. So never dismiss the ordinary, Mr. Clancy. It's the ordinary that counts the most in a very extraordinary manner."

Clancy nodded, dumbfounded.

"We'll be in touch," Mamudi said, turning to leave.

"Gentlemen," Clancy called to the four men as he left his farm, "I realize I'm not a professional soldier, but I have grown up in this part of the country. Please watch your backs at all times. You can never be too careful."

Buddha Chan turned and faced the barrel-chested man. "That, Mr. Clancy," he said, "goes without saying."

EIGHT

Kinski, Crazy Jack, Mamudi, and Buddha sat glumly around a table at the inn.

"We're halfway there." Kinski beamed, staring at his perfect hair in a shining goblet.

"Hooray," Jack muttered.

"What's the matter?" Buddha replied, scratching his massive stomach. "Things are going well."

"I don't like this whole setup." Jack sighed.

"Me, either," Mamudi said. "I understand your feelings. It's one thing to get involved in a war where there is clearly an evil side and a righteous side; it's something else again when both sides are trying to fight for age-old beliefs."

"I don't believe this," Kinski marveled. "We're here to fight the FSE! I'm hearing *Sunrise Semester* here!"

Jack scowled. "Mamudi's hit it on the nose, Kinski. Even if we do secure the guns for Shatterhand, we're not really going to be hurting the FSE directly. What we're going to be doing is hurting a lot of people who've been dug into their ways since before the FSE ever slithered to life. These people don't give a rat's ass who's supporting who . . . they're throwing Bibles at each other."

Buddha offered a small smile. "So who said war is supposed to make sense? Lobbing Bibles, mortars, dictators, czars, missles. War is always crazy. All you can do is hope the side you're on will eventually bring about sanity."

"Still," Jack said, downing a lager. "I'd feel better if there was a group that we could point at and say *there's* the bad guys."

49

"Wanna flip for it?" Kinski smirked.

"I vote for this buzzard," Buddha said, peering from above his glasses.

A tall, lean man marched toward them.

"My son tells me that you wanted to meet me," he announced from between chapped lips.

"We always like to meet new people." Jack shrugged. "We feel it makes us better, more well-rounded individuals."

"I'm William Woods," the gaunt man announced.

"Would you like a Scotch and soda?" Kinski asked.

"I wouldn't mind," Woods said.

"Then," Mamudi called to the barmaid. "A scotch 'n' soda for our new and distinguished friend."

"I'm not your *friend*," Woods muttered.

"That's right," Crazy Jack intoned. "You're not *anything* to us right about now."

"My son," William Woods began, "tells me that you're for hire."

"Maybe." Buddha chuckled, offering a sly, Oriental smile.

"How much will it *take*?" Woods countered. "I mean, I want those *Papists* out of the picture . . . for good."

"I believe we've returned to the religious aspect of life," Mamudi said with a sigh.

"Are you getting funny with me, Popeye?" Woods was simmering, and stared into Mamudi's glass orb.

"It doesn't actually *pop*." Mamudi smiled politely. "But I can rotate it between my thumb and forefinger."

"Who the hell are you bastards?" Woods demanded.

Buddha rested his pudgy chin on his chest. "Does it really matter, Mr. Woods? You can call us soldiers, mercenaries, samurai. Labels mean nothing. We are four men with certain skills. We have no country. We have no political affiliations. We are four men with certain skills attempting to get by."

"Gunslingers, eh?" Woods acknowledged with a crafty smile.

"Yeee-haw," Kinski said in a deliberately exaggerated Eastern European accent.

"And I suppose you'll work for anybody," Woods said, glaring at the men.

Jack smiled. "We *have* had an offer for our services," he acknowledged. "But we're not sure that we're going to take it."

"You listen to me," the FSE stooge continued. "I'm not going to be bullied into hiring men I don't know, I don't trust, and, frankly, I don't like. If you work for me, you'll take what I offer to pay you. I have very powerful friends behind me, and I have fifty of the best men in the area working for my interests full-time. Another hundred if I need them."

"Golly," Buddha said.

"All right," Woods said, standing. "Have it your way. But if you don't show up at my home by eight tonight, to pledge allegiance to the Woods cause, you won't be alive by nine. Don't even think of siding with the Clancys. They're dead men."

"For dead men"—Crazy Jack beamed—"they pay pretty well."

Woods stormed out of the inn.

"Now what?" Kinski asked.

"Well," Jack theorized, "I suppose we'll take an evening stroll, let's say, nine-ish?"

Kinski shook his well-combed head back and forth. "Have you found your bad guy?"

"Naaah," Jack replied, "but I've found someone I really don't like too much."

"Almost as good," Buddha acknowledged.

"I'll walk point," Mamudi said.

"We have a lot of, um, unpacking to do in the meantime," Buddha said.

"I do hope they like our rock 'n' roll ensembles," Kinski said, producing his ever-present comb and running it through his hair.

"Relax." Jack leaned back in his chair. "Dress is casual."

NINE

Freddie Mamudi staggered down a burned-out section of Feirgall. The buildings were scorched and pockmarked from years of fighting between neighbors. Merely shells of what used to be, now the surrounding streets looked like bad Hollywood sets from a psychedelic horror movie.

Mamudi talked loudly, drunkenly, into the midnight-blue fall sky.

"Deros by enny other name would smell so sweet," he called out, deros being a prewar term for the date a grunt was eligible for returning from overseas.

He remembered a funny little tune that one of his American uncles had taught him when he first made it to the States. It was from an old fifties show called *Winky Dink*. Mamudi launched into a full-tilt version of the song, substituting the words *dinky-dau*.

"Dinky-dau is me," he yodeled, "Dinky-dau is you. Dinky-dau is all of us together. . . ."

While he careened down the deserted, skeletal section of the village, he carefully scanned the area with his one good eye, the moon glistening off his skull-and-crossboned fake orb.

How could people with common ancestry do this to each other? he wondered.

Well, that was war biz.

"Dinky-dau," he continued to belch.

Diddy-bopping in an exaggerated manner down the shadow-strewn street, he felt the sweat begin to form at the tip of his zipper scar. He was in Indian country now, in a number-ten situation.

By the time the night was out, he might be up to triple digits in terms of sheer shit.

He sensed the noise before he actually heard it. An engine. Too powerful for a car. Truck, probably. Six-by, most likely. A flatbed. Wooden-slat sides. Carrying men.

In a way he was relieved. Exposing his presence the way he was, he was an easy mark for any sapper hiding in the ruins. Any farmboy who felt like busting caps could have cut him down in a second or less right about now.

And Mamudi was practically unarmed. No M16 slung over his shoulder tonight.

He wasn't merely walking point.

He was dangling bait.

His ass.

The Marauders had figured that Woods would try to stage something theatrical, something to teach both the quartet and the citizens of the town a lesson.

Mamudi smiled to himself. He had always prided himself in his teaching abilities.

Hanging beneath his parka was a compact mini-Uzi 9-mm SMG. Didn't weigh much, less than four pounds. Twenty-round magazines. Black plastic stock.

That would keep him afloat for a little while.

He heard the footsteps scurrying around him.

Woods's men were forming a U-shaped ambush.

He continued to sing and stagger, this time bursting into a rousing rendition of "What Do You Do with a Drunken Sailor," playing up his newly refurbished accent to the hilt.

"Whaddayooodooo wida drunchen say-loir," Mamudi bawled, trying desperately to make out the shapes around him in the darkness.

His world was suddenly flooded by bright, white light.

Headlights.

Mamudi staggered to a stop, swaying drunkenly in front of the blazing headlights. The flatbed truck roared up the street. Freddie continued to sway in place.

"Gennlemenz," he barked. "Start your enginzz."

The truck roared to a halt twenty yards away from Mamudi. A gangly figure leapt out.

But for the driver, the truck was deserted, Mamudi noticed.

The loping form marched forward. It was Willy Woods.

"My father missed you tonight, Popeye," the smirking youth called. "He didn't think it was too polite for you and your fellas to snub him like that."

"I yam what I yam and that's all what I yam," Mamudi sang by way of response, feeling more and more like this plan of Jack's wasn't exactly a hot idea.

He definitely wasn't playing Sergeant Rock tonight.

"We don't like foreigners much," Willy continued. "Especially *heatheners*."

Mamudi nodded dumbly, taking note of a small crater in the macadam not five feet from his left. It looked large enough to hold a man.

"Cat got your tongue, eh, *heathen*?" Willy chuckled. "Well, if you can't *talk* to entertain us, maybe you can *dance* just a tad for our personal pleasure."

Thirty men·emerged from the shadows in *U* formation. They cradled Sterling Mark 7s in their hands. Mamudi smiled inwardly; the Woodses weren't as green as they were cracked up to be.

The Mark 7 was called a pistol, but it was actually the grandson of the semiautomatic carbines used by the old United Kingdom troops during their dance across the Falklands.

The tubular-shaped weapon looked like something out of *Buck Rogers*, a 7.8-inch-barreled ray gun to end all ray guns.

Only instead of blasting rocket ships this evening, the spacemen would be aiming at Mamudi. Nine-millimeter parabellum rounds, Mamudi figured.

"So," Willy continued, "would you like to dance for us?"

Mamudi's mouth flapped open and closed a few times before he finally slurred, "I can't dance . . . exceptin' whirling-dervish tunes. Ya wouldn' happen to know enny, would ya?"

"We'll *improvise*," Willy said, nodding to his men.

The thugs began to strafe the concrete around Mamudi, sending up small, lethal frags of macadam and grit zinging through the air.

Mamudi exaggerated his movements. They were pissing around right about now, playing a deadly game.

Still, a game was a game.

Mamudi twisted and turned, pumping his legs up and down, flailing about like a chicken without a head while, beyond the spray, Willy's rodentlike laugh echoed hauntingly.

Mamudi did the dance.

The bullets zipped closer to his feet.

He danced his way toward the crater.

He had to play "target" for just a little while longer. Three-pronged attack. Outflank them. Monkey in the middle.

A bullet grazed Mamudi's left boot.

That was too close. He was too angry. That asshole, Willy, was laughing too hard.

He heard the jeep's horn bleat in the distance.

Sweat running down his bright red scar in spite of the cold, Mamudi executed a tuck-and-roll leap toward the crater, sprays of lead, concrete, and debris rising up all around him.

He whipped out the Uzi and swung it around in his right hand, firing a short burst in Willy's direction.

The slugs caught the laughing asshole just below the kneecaps, sending his high-pitched giggles into equally high-pitched screams of pain and surprise.

The wiry hayseed felt his legs give out from beneath him. He hit the ground, moaning, cursing, screeching.

His men, not fully comprehending the turnabout, continued firing at Mamudi.

Mamudi hunkered down in the small crater almost in a fetal position, unable to squeeze off a round.

He was pinned down on three sides with no chance of retreat.

Woods's goons, feeling cocky, began to march toward

the crater, spraying the small road with round after round of certain death.

Mamudi rubbed a piece of grit from his glass eye. "Bad move," he whispered.

"Rock and roll!" Crazy Jack's booming voice thundered from the darkness.

Mamudi shook his head, amused. He didn't know which was louder, Jack's voice or the roaring of the jeep.

Jack, driving with his left hand and wrapping his right arm around an M-60 machine gun, sent round after round smashing into Woods's startled unit.

Belts of ammo undulating wildly, Jack zeroed in on the rapidly scattering thugs.

Four slugs caught the apparent leader of the pack low in the belly. The man squealed like a pig and doubled over, his internal organs rapidly becoming external.

Jack sent the jeep into a wild semicircle, catching the startled men from all sides. Small horseshoe within a large horseshoe.

He continued to send bullets slamming into both flesh and brick, shattering one man's skull like a melon.

The men began a disorderly retreat toward their truck, firing their weapons at both the jeep and any shadow-shape they imagined.

Bullets sailed through the air like popcorn kernels over a superheated griddle.

Woods's goons hightailed it for the flatbed.

Willy lay ten yards away from the truck, still moaning, screaming, and bleeding.

From behind the truck, at the far end of the street, waddled the corpulent but formidable form of Buddha Chan. Over his shoulder he carried a Soviet/ChiCom RPG-2 rocket launcher, the old, reliable B-40. He dropped to one knee.

Woods's men ran for the truck, ignoring the screams of their would-be firgurehead.

"Where ya goin'," Willy screeched, "ya bastards, ya?"

Buddha peered into the night from behind his shades. He patted the smoothbore, muzzle-loaded weapon, 40-mm round, 84 meters per second velocity.

Buddha smiled. "Since you kids enjoy games," he whispered, "let's play Where'd My Fucking Truck Go?"

None of Woods's men were looking beyond the truck. Not one of them spotted the calm form of Buddha Chan.

Crazy Jack continued to spray at their heels.

Buddha let loose with a well-aimed, spin-stabilized round. The shell sizzled through the air and slammed into the rear of the truck, screeching into its gas tank.

The men running for the truck were astounded to watch the truck transform itself into a blazing fireball.

They skidded to a halt.

Time itself seemed to stop as the massive, roaring, angry fist of red, yellow, and orange thundered up toward the sky . . . before sprouting other fists, before reaching out toward the men.

The concussion of the explosion knocked a dozen men to the ground, which saved their lives. The rest were caught by the titanic, ever-spreading fireball.

Their skin sizzled.

Their throats were invaded by white-hot blades of suffocating pain. Eyes disappeared. Organs popped. Their clothing remained only as an afterthought.

The men tried to force screams out of their charred lungs. All that emerged were short, gasping, hissing sounds.

Within an instant it was over.

Most of Woods's men were over.

Jack swung the jeep around to Mamudi. Mamudi was still crouched in his crater, his hair slightly singed from the explosion.

"Taxi?" Jack asked.

Mamudi leapt into the jeep, rubbing his hand through his hair, sending small slivers of burned curlicues cascading down onto his shoulder. "Can't Buddha be more careful?"

Jack shrugged, glancing at Mamudi's new hairdo. "What? What's the matter? I like it. It's very *now*. It's very *you*!"

Jack roared like a madman, sending the jeep speeding after the retreating dozen men.

Woods's dirty dozen skittered off the street and darted through the deserted ruins of religious wars gone by. They fired their Mark-7s back in the direction of Jack and Mamudi.

Jack pulled the jeep up to curbside.

"They're going to get away!" Mamudi exclaimed.

Jack slid out of the jeep and slowly, casually began picking up whatever salvageable pistols he could find in the street. "Naaah," he said with a shrug.

From a distance Mamudi heard the familiar sound of Kinski's AK-47.

Kinski's salvo was returned by scattered cap-busting.

The AK-47 sparked to life again.

This time there was no return fire.

A minute later Kinski strode out from the long dormant ruins of the shattered side of Feirgall. Jack was busy piling the pistols in the jeep. "Any survivors?" he asked.

"Are you kidding?" Kinski asked. "Half of them shot each other."

Mamudi still sat in the jeep, removing slivers of singed hair from his scalp.

Kinski offered him a comb. "I like it," he said. "Very butch."

Mamudi muttered an ancient, heartfelt, and very dark oath under his breath as Buddha Chan marched over, placing the B-40 in the back of the jeep. "You did very well, Mamudi," he said. "I never knew you could dance like that, you dervish, you."

Mamudi found yet another euphemism for a biologically impossible act in his litany of ancestral sayings and slid out of the jeep.

Jack pointed to the still shrieking, wiry form of Willy Woods.

"Let's get Junior over there and pay a visit on his proud papa."

Mamudi glanced at the screeching young man. He then looked at the torn toe of his left boot. "With pleasure."

Mamudi walked over to the sweating, squirming youth. "Hello." He grinned. "Remember me?"

"Help me, sweet Jesus," Willy said, moaning. "I hurt. I hurt so *bad*."

"The name is not Jesus." Mamudi smiled. "It's Mamudi, your *heathen* friend. Let me tell you something about my heathenism," he said, his good eye glaring at the boy, his death's-head orb shining down at the frightened youth's face.

"Over the years my beliefs have produced poets, prophets, and governments. We were, we *are,* mystical people. In the Koran, the mystics found that God 'loves them and they loved him.' In fact, by paying attention to the rules of God, we could attain *ikhlas*, absolute purity of intention and act. Isn't that remarkable?"

"My fuggin' legs are bleeding!" Willy philosophized.

Mamudi ignored him. "My heathen ways are rich and layered. The world and God were said to be like that of ice and water, or perhaps like two mirrors contemplating themselves in each other, joined in a beatific union."

"I'm dying here, yer pig!"

Mamudi grinned at the squirming punk. "The Prophet Muhammad was said to be the universal man, the perfect man, the perfect physical manifestation of the divine names, the prototype of creation. He is the 'word.' The model for the spiritual realization of the possibilities of man."

"Bugger off!"

"You, however," Mamudi said, gazing down at his sliced boot, "are a real sack of shit."

Mamudi brought back his boot and kicked little Willy directly in the stomach. The boy bellowed in pain and lapsed into unconsciousness.

"Someday," Mamudi whispered, "I will explain to you about the union of God and man in the hereafter. For now, if you ever swear at me again, I will teach you of the union of knife blade and belly."

Mamudi walked back toward the jeep, his zipper scar beet-red.

"I thought you were going to fetch Junior," Crazy Jack asked.

Mamudi jumped into the jeep. "I'm a fighter, not a janitor," he said, seething.

Jack, never actually seeing Mamudi angry before, backed off.

"Damn," he said, walking back to the unconscious boy. "I have to do *every* goddamn thing around here myself."

Jack bent over and lifted the boy over his left shoulder as if the bleeding kid were a sack of potatoes.

He marched back toward the vehicle, muttering, "I've got religious assholes to the left of me, to the right of me, and now I'm fighting alongside one. Jeez, if I had been smart, I woulda opted for the goddamn CIA, or at least the National Guard. By now I could have been a president or something, maybe a vice president. I woulda settled for that."

He tossed the deadweight into the back of the jeep, between Mamudi and Buddha, and climbed behind the wheel.

"Now, if it doesn't *offend* one of you, would you please rip a couple of strips off your goddamn shirts and tie tourniquets around this slimy little bastard's legs before we lose our live bargaining chip and wind up with one fuggin' dead piece of meat?"

Mamudi stared grimly ahead. "I refuse to touch the ignorant weasel."

Buddha sighed and, reaching inside his parka, pulled out two large bandannas.

As Jack cranked up the jeep, Buddha bent over the boy. "Okay, sonny, we're going get you all patched up so you can help us light up a very big fuse."

Willy Woods came to at that point. "Fuck you, chink."

"Mongol," Buddha said, simmering, before letting go with a left hook that knocked the witless Willy even more so.

Kinski didn't bother to turn around. "See what I mean?"

TEN

Crazy Jack guided the jeep through the darkness, Willy Woods moaning in the back.

"The little prick sounds like a cat in a blender," he muttered.

"The wounds were clean too," Buddha added.

Mamudi smiled thinly, removing his death's-head eye and reaching inside his vest for a new orb, one bearing the SEAL insignia. "Of course. If I had wanted to kill him, I would have. I just wanted to give him a taste."

Jack pulled the jeep over to the side of a small dirt road. "What's up?" Kinski asked.

"We're splitting up," Crazy Jack said. "We're going to give the Woodses something to think about."

Jack leapt out of the jeep, turning to Mamudi. "How would you like a nice evening stroll, my nature-loving friend?"

Mamudi shrugged, grabbing a Mark 7 and some ammo from the back. "I'm not going to have to dance, am I?" he asked.

Jack grinned and pulled out an Armalite AR-180 from the jeep. "Nope. This time *we're* going to call the tune."

Buddha jumped behind the wheel. "Jack?"

Keenan grinned at him sheepishly. "You two fellows bring Mamudi's sack of shit back to Woods and negotiate. Freddie and I are going to settle a score."

Kinski ran a hand through his golden locks. "Unfinished business from the old war?"

Jack winked at him. "Call me an asshole, but I think we

can do some good, as well as take advantage of an existing situation."

Kinski grinned. "You're an asshole." His smile faded and Kinski returned the wink. "But I *do* understand."

Jack reached inside the jeep and yanked out the RPG-2 rocket launcher. He glanced at Buddha. "Don't worry, I'll bring it back."

"I never worry." Buddha nodded. "Bad for the digestive track."

Jack motioned to Mamudi. The pair double-timed it across a dark, fog-enshrouded field.

Willy Woods stirred in the backseat. "What the hell is going on here?" he mumbled. "I hurt. I hurt so bad."

Buddha Chan tilted his glasses down to the tip of his round nose. "Just consider us a taxi service, sonny. Just tell us how to take you home."

Young, blond Molly McGuire sat listlessly in the small bed that had been provided for her by Willy Woods. A half dozen armed guards sat around the living room outside her chambers, their Viking submachine guns in hand.

The Vikings came into vogue before the war. Virginia models. Made just outside D.C. in the States, right under the nose of the Pentagon. Fired thirty-six 9-mm shells, they did. Lighter than an Uzi, with stock extended the powerful little suckers were less than twenty-three inches in length.

The guns came courtesy of an FSE score a year before wherein the Woods clan was heavily rewarded for their intelligence operations.

The men within the cottage were confident. Even over-confident. There wasn't anyone around Feirgall who was so well armed.

No one they knew about, at any rate.

Outside the small cottage, two identically armed guards patrolled the area.

Blustering MacMillan was there, in all his bulldog glory.

Across from the cottage, in her own humble abode, old Mrs. McGuire watched hopelessly as the guards marched back and forth in front of her daughter's prison.

Then she saw the massive stranger with the fiery red hair amble down the road.

"Who goes there?" MacMillan demanded, aiming his pistol at Crazy Jack. His runty companion sidled up to MacMillan, flashing a freckled sneer.

Jack continued to march forward, his RPG-2 slung casually over his shoulder, fully loaded.

"I said," MacMillan growled, "who goes there?"

"Nobody much." Jack grinned. "Just your worst fucking nightmare."

The two guards ran forward, one after the other, a tremendously stupid tactical move.

"Stop or I'll shoot," MacMillan barked.

"Say good night, Gracie," Crazy Jack hissed, letting go with a massive 40-mm round.

Mrs. McGuire watched in astonishment as the orange-haired titan sent what looked to her like an airborne, albeit Lilliputian, torpedo screaming through the air.

The rocket slammed into both MacMillan and his crony behind him. The men had time to scream like banshees as their bodies exploded around them. A blast of red-hot light. Smoke. Ashes. There wasn't much to see after that.

Dense smoke.

Flickering tongues of flame.

Mrs. McGuire ducked down in her living room as the barred windows shook fiercely, as if fondled by a benign thunderbolt.

After a few seconds she scrambled to her feet. She peered out of the window. The giant had disappeared behind the wall of smoke.

MacMillan and the other guard had disappeared.

All that remained were two pairs of shoes, two weapons, and small, red slices of objects she didn't really want to think about.

The six guards scrambled out of her daughter's prison house, yelling in confusion, training their weapons on anything that promised to move.

Unfortunately for the guards, there wasn't anything moving outside the house.

They turned and ran toward Molly McGuire's prison-cottage.

The door slammed shut, latched securely from the inside. "What the hell is going on in there, bitch!" one of the guards yelled.

"That is no way to talk to a woman" came a voice from the darkness. "In the writings of Ibn al-Arabi and Ibn al-Farid, eternal beauty is symbolized through female beauty."

A series of shots rang out.

Two guards fell, reeling. The calm voice continued. "In Indo-Muslim mystical songs, the eternal soul is found in the soul of a loving wife, God the longed-for husband."

There was a click of another cartridge being slapped into place.

The remaining guards began to sweat, fanning their silent muzzles this way and that, watching for any shadow-shape to form.

One guard decided to open up on an adjacent field of barley.

He succeeded in snapping several yards of barley in two.

Many future shots of whiskey died in his shooting.

Silence.

Another volley.

Two guards felt their necks explode. They dropped their weapons, their arms instinctively reaching up for their heads . . . heads that were no longer there.

Their twitching fingers grasped at the air, their bodies shaking and shivering.

They turn and spun round and round, their heads lying at their feet.

The men finally collapsed in a heap, disgorging blood in vast, pumping upheavals.

Mamudi stepped out of the darkness. "In fact, one of the greatest contributions of Sufism to Islamic literature is *poetry.*"

The two remaining guards gaped at the scarred, one-eyed, slightly singed Marauder.

They tried to fire at Mamudi from the hip.

Mamudi allowed them to attempt the maneuver.

He gave them three seconds.

The guards sent their bullets spraying wildly. Mamudi hit the roadside and carefully aimed the Mark 7 at the two men's midsections. He used the entire cartridge.

The two men teeter-tottered above the ground, nearly sliced in two.

Glancing at each other one last time, the two thugs slammed down onto the street.

Inside Molly McGuire's prison, Jack calmly kicked in the back door. Glancing around the nearly abandoned shack, he came to the bedroom. He made a move to open the door and then thought better of it.

He gently knocked on the bedroom door. "Miss McGuire?"

"Go away" came a trembling voice.

"I'm here to help you," Jack replied.

He eased the door open. A frightened, disheveled Molly McGuire sat on the bed, hugging her legs beneath her quivering chin.

"Who are you?" she demanded. "Did Willy send you here to have a crack at me too?"

Jack stared at the young woman. So young, yet so hardened. Well, maybe there was time to reverse the process.

He knelt gently at the side of her bed. "No, he didn't. Listen to me. You don't have much time, so pay attention to everything I say. I'm not here to hurt you. I know what you've been through and I can't undo that. I know it. But as of now, you're free."

"I want to see that bastard dead," Molly said. "What he did to my father . . . my mother . . . to me . . ."

"Well, you *can't* see the bastard dead. It wouldn't be smart or safe. Rest assured that he will die, and soon. It's going to be hard and it's going to hurt a hell of a lot, but I want you to leave here now. Head south. Once you cross the border, go to the nearest police station. By the time you reach there, I'm sure you'll be given sanctuary. Mention the name the Marauders. You'll be safe, I promise."

He reached into his pocket and pulled out eight five-pound notes. "This should get you there. Stay off the main roads."

"Why are you doing this?"

Jack offered a shy smile. "Because I *can*."

Molly gave him a quizzical look. "I don't understand."

"You don't have to. Now, can you use a gun?"

"My father had a shotgun once."

He handed her a .45 Colt. "I'll show you how to fire this outside. Keep it hidden and only use it if you have to. If anyone bothers you in any way, wait until they are within five feet of you, and then point it at their belly, understand?"

Molly nodded. Jack led the startled woman outside and showed her how to lock and unlock the safety on the gun.

Mamudi stepped out of the shadows.

Molly made a move to raise the Colt.

Jack restrained her. "You learn quickly, but he's on *your* side."

"Freddie Mamudi," the smiling man said, bowing, "at your service."

"Molly McGuire." She nodded.

"You're . . . not married, are you?" Mamudi said, winking his good eye.

"Mamudi," Jack said with a groan, "she's just leaving."

"Molly!" cried a tiny voice. "Molly, my dearie."

Old Mrs. McGuire, her thin legs churning, her stockings bunched around her ankles, sprinted across the road and wrapped her skeletal arms around her only child.

"The saints preserve us, I never thought I'd see you leave that place without the scum of the Woodses attached to your arms," she said, weeping.

Molly McGuire hugged her tiny mother. "T-these men," Molly stammered, "they *saved* me."

"I know, I know." Mrs. McGuire sobbed. "Your guardian angels, they are. I saw them this morning. It was as if the Good Lord himself placed them here: a one-eyed prophet and a lovely giant with the hair of St. Patrick."

Both Crazy Jack and Mamudi shuffled their feet.

"They want me to go south, Ma," Molly said. "There'll be freedom there . . . for both of us."

Crazy Jack nodded. "Our people will be there, Mrs. McGuire. It would be a good idea for you to go with your daughter. She has a firearm. She knows how to use it."

"Firearm?" Mrs. McGuire said, pointing to the Colt. "You call *that* a gun? I've been using shotguns since I was a wee one. You should have seen my husband handle a shotgun; he could pepper a crowd of two dozen in a second of more. A World War II veteran he was, and his father a decorated hero of the War to End All Wars."

"All the same, Mrs. McGuire—" Mamudi began.

"Now, don't be fretting over me, Towel-head, no offense intended," she replied.

"None taken." Mamudi grinned. He hadn't heard *that* slur in years.

Mrs. McGuire studied Mamudi's face. "And what caused that terrible wound on your kisser?"

Mamudi found himself liking the spindly elderly woman. Three decades ago she would have made a fine wife. "A Russian sniper, ma'am."

"I'm no one's ma'am," the old woman replied. "I'm just a woman, a mother. Got a lot of years left in me yet. So the dirty Red bastards did that to ya, did they? Well, if I had been around, I would have taken off their bloody heads."

"I'm sure you would have . . . Mrs. McGuire," Mamudi said.

"You can bet your blessed butt on that one." Mrs. McGuire smirked. "Now, as to me leaving with my daughter, here, I'll hear none of it. You rescued her. We're both beholden to you. But her life is ahead of her. Mine is behind me now. *She* should be the one who goes to true Ireland. As for myself, I could never leave here. This is my ancestral home. My father was born here and his father and his father's father. I'll not be leaving here on account of those flatworms known as Woodses."

"But, Ma'am . . . Mrs. McGuire," Crazy Jack pleaded, "you won't be *safe* here, especially after Molly . . . I mean, your daughter, has been freed."

Mrs. McGuire screwed up her prunelike face into an impish grin. "What? What's that you say? A poor, half-deaf, and mostly blind widow like me not hearing or seeing a thing in the middle of the night? Why, it seems to me that any sane man would realize that it's just quite likely I slept on through all the commotion."

Crazy Jack sympathized, but still couldn't agree with the elderly woman. "Excuse me, ma'am, but I'm not sure that we're dealing with sane men, here."

"I realize that, big fellow." She smiled grimly. "But I'm not about to let those bastards off the hook. My husband and I were married for forty years. We lost two sons. Molly was our youngest, and last, child.

"We took great pride in her. Wanted to have a good life. Then the Big War happened. People, leaders we had never heard of, never thought about, decided to try to destroy the world. Well, we survived. We did the best we could. We have survived the troubles for all these years.

"We knew we could survive anything. We got our home back into shape. Watched the town get back on its feet. And then, after all that, I had to watch my husband be slaughtered because of one pimply-faced squirt!

"No." She shook her head. "Molly's place is in free Ireland. My place is here. I would never leave my husband. I will wait to die until I see my husband's killer cold in his grave. I've spoken. That's what I will do."

"Oh, Mama," Molly cried, embracing her mother. Both the women wept. In truth both Crazy Jack and Mamudi were close to tears as well.

It was the mother who broke the embrace. "Now, away with ye, child. Head toward Freedomland. Do as the big man told you, and please, be careful when you use the pistol. It'll probably have a kick like a mule. Be careful who you wield it against, and be careful who you show it to."

"I will, Mama," Molly said.

"Now go along. Head south. May your days be very happy. May your life be free from cares. May St. Patrick ask Our Blessed Lord to answer all your prayers."

Mrs. McGuire gave Molly a kiss on the cheek. The old woman turned then, and returned to her home.

"I have to be getting my beauty sleep. I haven't seen nor heard a blessed thing."

The old woman toddled into her house and slammed the front door behind her.

Molly turned toward Crazy Jack and Mamudi.

"You'd best do as your mother said," Crazy Jack said.

Molly nodded and, tucking the gun deep within her skirt waistband, walked off down the road.

"Let's get the hell out of here," Crazy Jack said.

Jack and Mamudi jogged off the road and ran, full-tilt, across the barley field toward the Woodses' house.

ELEVEN

Buddha Chan pulled the jeep up in front of the Woods home, a large, thatched-roof structure at least three hundred years old. From the outside it looked like the kind of house that Peter Rabbit might have lived in but on a slightly grander scale. There were two guards posted in front of a picket fence.

They didn't seem too happy to see the jeep.

Which made Buddha feel happy.

"Don't use your weapon unless you have to," he said to Kinski. Kinski nodded and slung the AR-180 over his shoulder. It was the perfect weapon for fighting on the run. Kinski hoped they wouldn't be doing much running.

Buddha stopped the jeep directly before the front gate. He stepped outside and tossed the moaning Willy Woods over his shoulder and marched forward.

The two guards raised their weapons as Buddha took the lead. "State your business," the first guard snarled, a strapping young man standing at least six inches taller than Buddha.

"We're delivering something for Mr. Woods," Buddha said.

The larger of the two guards walked up to Buddha and stared down at his round, shaved head. He took in Willy Woods's ashen, sweaty face. "We'll take it from here, chink."

Buddha peered up into the man's blotched face from behind his shooter's glasses. "We'd prefer to make the delivery ourselves. We have certain matters to discuss."

"I said we'd take it from here," the first guard replied, cradling his rifle in one hand and reaching forward toward Buddha.

Buddha's movements were so quick that not even Kinski could be sure of what he was seeing, let alone the two guards. Buddha grabbed on to the guard's extended hand and snapped it back. As the man backed up, howling in pain, the rotund Buddha, Willy still over his shoulder, leapt into the air.

He kicked out with his left foot, making contact with the stunned guard. Still airborne, Buddha kicked through the mist with his right foot.

The left foot slammed into the man's right leg, just below the kneecap.

The guard hissed as he felt his right leg give out. His body began to topple forward toward Buddha. The round Marauder's right foot slammed into the guard's stomach, effectively knocking the wind out of him, doubling him over and giving him a lot to think about.

Buddha's left hand, flattened out in karate mode, came down hard on the base of the man's neck.

The man collapsed in a heap before Buddha's feet.

The second guard, a thin, angry young whelp, decided to charge Buddha and leap on him in what almost seemed to be an NFL tackle.

Buddha bent his knees and crouched low to the ground, sumo-style. As the young guard sailed toward him, Buddha squatted, allowing the boy to half pass over his head. He then reached up with his free hand and, extending his five pudgy fingers, snapped them shut around the leaping lout's balls. Once he had ensnared the stupefied sentry's scrotum, Buddha squeezed hard and, raising his arm high in the air, stood up straight.

He held the screaming, squirming man high over his head. Kinski almost laughed. It looked like a ballet for sado-masochists.

Buddha stared up at the wriggling, would-be tough guy. "Drop the gun or join the Vienna Boys Choir for life." He smiled sweetly.

Sweat dripping down and off his nose, the grimacing

goon allowed his gun to drop the ground. "Please," he squeaked, "please."

Buddha smiled and lowered the lad to the ground. "One of life's magic words. Do you know the other one?"

The gasping guard lay on the ground, holding his savaged scrotum. "Thank you," he whispered. "Thank you."

Kinski marveled at Buddha's catlike grace, as well as his sense of cool. "How did you *do* that?"

Buddha shrugged. "People are polite at heart. You just have to encourage them. Remember *Mr. Rogers' Neighborhood*?"

"I didn't mean it like that." Kinski laughed.

"I know it," Buddha replied, straightening his glasses.

Kinski smiled. "Let's see Mr. Woods."

The two men marched toward the house with Buddha dallying for a moment over the unconscious first guard. "And don't ever try touching me again," he whispered.

Buddha calmly knocked on the front door. A beaming William Woods swung it open. "Well, Royce, I hope you taught those bas—"

". . . tards?" Kinski said, kicking the door open.

"We brought you a present," Buddha said, walking by the stunned, stringy form of William Woods and easing young Willy down onto the couch.

"What have you done to my son!" Woods demanded.

"Looks like we shot him," Buddha said.

"It's not serious," Kinski said.

"But he won't be doing a jig for a while," Buddha said.

"I could kill you for this!" Woods said, seething, standing over his son.

"You could *try*," Buddha replied with a shrug.

"But before you do that, I'd ask the rest of the men you sent just how good we are at keeping people from taking us out," Kinski advised.

Woods glanced around the room, confused.

Kinski snapped his fingers. "Oh, that's right, you *can't* ask the rest of your men."

"And why's that?" Woods asked.

"They're dead," Buddha said flatly.

"Now, Mr. Woods," Kinski said, "are we going to talk a deal or what?"

"I—I can get plenty more men," Woods muttered.

"What's the point?" Kinski replied. "You send them up against us and it'll be the same story."

"History does have a way of repeating itself," Buddha said.

"There were four of you," Woods said suspiciously, "and now I see but *two*."

A serpent's grin appeared on the man's face. "How do I know that you're telling me the truth? How do I know that my men don't have your two friends in their clutches right now?"

"Because the other two are at your back," a voice boomed from the kitchen of the house.

Woods spun around as Crazy Jack and Mamudi, sweat glistening on their faces, stepped into the living room.

"It's not hard to outflank your men," Mamudi offered.

"Sorry about the back door too," Jack added. "But you needed a sturdier lock, anyway."

Woods's world began to spin. "You can't just come in here and take over my operation," he said. "I have the FSE's guaranteed support."

"We don't want to take over," Jack offered.

"And if you're talking about that local FSE operative," Kinski said, producing a comb and adjusting his front wave, "we hear he's a weasely little runt. If we could take on your men, I don't think we'll have too much trouble taking out one operative."

"The thing is, Mr. Woods," Buddha said soothingly, "we're not out to do you in. Frankly, we tend not to stay in one place for a very long time."

"Local politics don't interest us," Mamudi stated.

"We're citizens of the world, friend." Jack smiled. "Just four fellows out to put their talents to use. Take a job. Get paid. Move on."

"But how do I know I can trust you?" Woods asked.

"Frankly, I think it's *us* who should be asking *you* that question."

Woods had no reply.

"Look," Kinski said. "It comes down to this. You know, and the Clancys know, about the arms shipment. It's just a matter of who gets the arms first. The winner will heat up your little feud and probably wind up winning it, at least for a while.

"Now you have a choice. You can hire us and get *your* hands on those guns or whatever, or Clancy can hire us . . . and he'll win the big prize. It's that simple."

"Of course, we'll have to negotiate," Jack said.

Scratching his brow above the glass eye, Mamudi said, "We were thinking of seventy-five thousand pounds and fifteen percent of whatever we take."

Woods shook his head. "Too much," he said. "Even for the likes of you. Sixty thousand and twelve percent is as high as I'll go . . . but I'm not convinced that I should take the chance of hiring you. What proof do I have that you'll be loyal to me?"

"We won't be." Jack shrugged.

"But we'll be loyal to the sixty thousand and twelve percent," Kinski pointed out.

Woods ran a gnarled hand across his chin. "I'm still not sure. My cause has managed to keep the Clancys and their kind in check for generations. I'm not sure that you'd make a difference one way or the other.

"You say you killed my men tonight. Fine. But I can replace those twenty with twenty times twenty more, and twenty times twenty after that."

"It's hard to argue against that kind of logic." Buddha shrugged.

"Mr. Woods doesn't function on logic," Crazy Jack said, staring at the Irishman. "If he did, he never would have sent his men out on a stupid revenge mission. Instead, he would have put them to better use in his war against the Clancy men. He would have been concentrating on the arms shipment. He wouldn't have used his men as toys."

"They are *my* men," Woods replied.

"They *were* your men," Jack growled. "They're maggot meals now."

"Let's go," Mamudi said. "We'll give Mr. Woods some time to decide."

They turned to leave the house. "One thing to think about, Mr. Woods," Jack said before making a move to exit the room. "You may have held the Clancys back for years, but as a soldier, let me tell you an interesting fact of warfare, sort of a peek into the psychological side of fighting.

"If you fight with your back against the wall long enough, you start to get tired of it. Then you start to get mad about it. Then, when you're mad enough and you know you have nothing to lose, you're willing to take chances that no sane man ever would. You try to do the most damage to the enemy you can before they take you out.

"And the funny thing is, a lot of times they *don't* take you out. They're caught by surprise. They're amazed at your ferocity. They're still playing by the old rules, and here you are making up rules as you go along.

"That's a very dangerous situation to be in, Mr. Woods. Just be advised."

Woods snorted, a wicked smile appearing on his face. "You're not actually trying to tell me that after all this time the Clancys have the guts or the gumption to rally against me, are you?"

"I'm not telling you anything," Jack said, turning his back on the man. "I just thought I'd recount what I believed was an interesting bit of combat trivia. Good night, Mr. Woods."

At that point one of Woods's men dashed through the front door, breathless. The young man skittered past the Marauders and stumbled to a stop in front of Woods.

Woods wasn't pleased at the intrusion. "What is it, Donald?"

"It's Molly, Mr. Woods. It's Willy's girl!"

"What about her?"

"She's gone."

"What? She ran away?"

"No, sir, not exactly," the boy said, shamefaced.

"Well, what happened to her?" Woods demanded.

"We're not sure, sir."

"Bring MacMillan to me, then."

"We can't, sir."

"Why not?"

The boy shuffled his feet. "Uh, he's gone too."

Woods rolled his eyes. "And you're not sure where he's gone, either, eh?"

"No," the boy replied. "We're sure about what happened to him. He's, well, he's gone to sit at the right hand of God Almighty, sir."

Woods was aghast. "Mac is *dead*? How did it happen?"

The boy cleared his throat. "He seems to have exploded, Mr. Woods."

"Ex—"

"Mr. O'Donnell seems to have been blown up as well. As for the Evans boys, they lost their heads. Frankie Wright was sliced in two, just about, and so . . ."

"All the men guarding that little whore were killed?" Woods yelled.

"*Slaughtered* would be a better word, sir," the boy said.

Woods stared at the Marauders. "Did *you* . . ."

Jack shrugged. "Don't look at us, we were busy with your toy soldiers."

Woods sat, seething. "Those sons of bitches Clancys!"

He sat in silence for a moment.

He raised his head and faced the Marauders.

"You're hired" was all he said.

TWELVE

The Marauders returned to Barney's Inn and trudged up to their two rooms. "I think I should make a call," Jack said with a sigh.

"Five will get you ten there are more bugs on our phones than in most New York tenements." Kinski smirked.

"No problem," Crazy Jack said. "We have Shatterhand's private number, right?"

"Yeah"—Buddha shrugged—"so what?"

"So I'll just call my cousin and talk to him in jargon these plowboys won't understand," Jack replied.

Mamudi and Jack entered one room, while Buddha and Kinski strolled toward another. "Do you think they have blow dryers in this dive?" Kinski thought aloud.

"I couldn't care less." Buddha sighed. "The last haircut I had resembled a quick buff job."

Jack and Mamudi entered the small room. Mamudi collapsed on the bed, still mourning the wounding of one perfectly swell boot.

Jack walked over to the phone and dialed the area code for London. The phone rang in the U.K.'s short beep-beep, beep-beep series.

A familiar voice, albeit a groggy one, barked over the line, "Who the hell is this?"

"Cuz?" Jack said. "You'll never guess who this is."

"Jeezus, whoever it is, do you have any idea what time it is?"

"It's your cousin, Jack!" Keenan exclaimed.

Silence.

On the other end of the line, King Shatterhand snapped to.

"Jackie?" he exclaimed. "Little Jackie!"

"Not so little anymore," Jack said, playing up the family reunion for all who could be listening. "I'm a big boy now, with lots and lots of responsibilities."

"Why, I haven't seen you since before the war," Shatterhand said. "When I visited you in California and we went to Ditzyland."

"Disneyland," Jack corrected. "I thought we should get together in a week or two."

"Sounds fine to me, Jackie. Where are you now?"

"A little town in Northern Ireland. I have some business up here. And right about now it looks like business will be booming soon."

"I'm glad to hear it," Shatterhand noted.

"Funny, I was just thinking about the old days, when we used to listen to music. The job would go a lot faster up here if I had an LP. Spin a few platters. Stereo sound."

Shatterhand thought hard, scanning his memory for what LP *really* meant. A listening post, he concluded. Jack wanted a forward observation post consisting of a couple of good men in place in Londonderry to monitor all ships leaving and entering the area.

"I'd *love* to send you one," Shatterhand replied. "I guess I could get it over to you in a couple of days. The mail service has improved a lot around here in the last year or so."

"Great," Jack replied. "This is a really interesting place, cuz. I miss old bouncing Betty, but there's enough ladies up here to allow me to replace her in my heart. I think Charlie will be impressed if I can introduce him to one or two Betty babes."

Shatterhand was silent for a long second, putting the message together. A bouncing Betty was a bobby-trapped mine that was designed to spring up out of the ground after being tripped and explode about three feet away from the surface, slicing into a man at waist level. Charlie was an old Vietnam term for enemy. Jack was going to shake things up through some old guerrilla tactics.

"I'm sure Charlie will be impressed. Tell him I said hi in a very big way," Shatterhand answered. "How have you enjoyed your stay in the U.K. so far?"

"Well, cuz, it reminds me of the *Indian Country* I've visited. A lot of kids *busting caps* in the streets, but they're pretty harmless. We took a walk through the *bush* tonight, and it was very peaceful, if you get my *point*. It was an exhausting stroll, and all in all, we wound up *wasting* a lot of time. It reminded me of our old times, real *rock and roll* scenes. My friend Freddie found a *spider hole* and he really had a great time. My friend Chan loves the place. The water's nearby and you know how he loves *sailing*. And, oh yeah, my friend Freddie has gotten to pig out on *K-bars* and that kind of *sharp* stuff. As for my friend Kinski? He's been acting like a real *sap*. I don't think he'll break out of it, either."

Shatterhand's mind reeled. "I think I should be writing all this down," he said with forced jocularity.

Shatterhand thought hard. The Marauders were definitely in enemy territory. A lot of local yokels had tried to ambush them. Apparently unsuccessfully. The Marauders had gone into the territory and wound up slaughtering a lot of FSE stooges, largely because of the forward scout, probably Mamudi. He had managed to find a small spot in the ground to dig in deep and send a lot of automatic or semi-automatic rounds into his attackers.

Chan had been using his martial-arts skills and Mamudi had used his knife prowess at least once.

Kinski, meanwhile, had been shooting effectively, taking the enemy by surprise.

"I'm glad you like the turf." Shatterhand chuckled.

"It's like a fairy tale come true," Jack replied. "It's like the old story about the princess who leaves her land for another and needs a knight or two to protect her."

Shatterhand couldn't decipher that one. "I don't remember that."

"Come on, cuz," Jack chided. "You remember that one. We were both kids. Once upon a time there was a wonderful land with a beautiful princess who wasn't happy there. She decided to leave her kingdom and head toward a more peaceful one, where there were no wars. No *trouble*."

Shatterhand sighed. Jack had gotten personally involved. "Is that the one where the kindly knight risks his entire career on getting her out of her kingdom and where his brother knight rides to her rescue to lead her into a safer, more idyllic land?"

"Exactly," Jack replied.

Shatterhand was fuming. "But she had to run a real gauntlet of horrors."

"But the knight had given her a magic sword, which he taught her how to use. Because it was magic, however, the princess could only use it so many times *a clip*. I'm sorry that's slang. Just so many times before the magic wore off."

"I remember the story well," Shatterhand mumbled. "But I can't remember the princess's name. Was it Guinevere?"

"Jeez, cuz," Jack said, "you know how bad I am with names. Gretel? Grendel? Heidi? *Molly*? They all sound the same to me. Well, I have to be getting to my work, cuz. I'll talk to you soon, okay?"

"Okay, Jackie." Shatterhand sighed. "I'll be sure to keep the fairy tale in mind when I'm on the road. It'll be something to keep my mind from wandering. What's your number up there, if I want to chat some more?"

Jack gave Shatterhand the number and extension of his room. "I hope to hear from you soon, cuz."

"If not from me," Shatterhand said, signing off, "you'll be hearing from one of my family about getting you the LP you wanted. Any particular type of music?"

"Well, I've always loved rock and roll," Jack said.

"You've got it," Shatterhand stated.

Jack hung up the phone.

Mamudi flopped over in the bed. "Do you think he got it all?"

"Oh, sure," Jack replied, sitting down on his bed.

"Did he have anything to say?"

"Nothing much." Jack shrugged. "You know how relatives are."

THIRTEEN

The Marauders sat in Barney's the following morning eating breakfast when barrel-chested Thomas Clancy sauntered in. He joined them, without invitation, at their table.

"How goes it?" he asked.

"As fine as can be expected," Jack replied between forkfuls of runny scrambled eggs.

"Has the Woods clan taken you in as yet?" Clancy queried.

"They have," Jack answered.

"Don't turn around," Buddha advised, "but two of Woods's men are at the far side of the pub. I recognize the little fellow from last night. He was the one who ran in breathless at the end of the negotiations."

Clancy nodded. "Have you heard what happened last night?"

"About the McGuire girl?" Mamudi answered.

"Indeed, just that," Clancy said. "You're going to have to work overtime to keep the Woods gang from our throats. I'm sure they suspect *us* as having freed her."

"I did too," Kinski said.

"No," Clancy said. "It must have been some of the locals. I'm glad of it, mind you, but I'm afeared that Woodses will be after retribution."

Jack nodded sagely. "All right, then. We'll have to stage a scene here. You want Woods to think that we're rejecting your offer, right?"

"Right."

"And you want us to cozy up to Woods and spill everything we learn to you."

"That's the plan," Clancy said enthusiastically.

"Then here's what you'll have to do," Jack said. "We won't be available to protect you should Woods decide to garner some payback for the McGuire girl. You'll have to call in every man who's on your side. Double your guards; triple your firepower if you can."

"That won't be hard. I can send runners to the neighboring villages," Clancy said.

"Then do just that," Jack replied. "We'll keep a careful watch on Woods and an open ear about the shipment of guns."

"You're a good lad, Jack," Clancy replied.

"And now," Jack said, "you'll have to forgive me for what I'm going to do."

Clancy blinked.

Jack leapt to his feet. "Get the hell out of here, you scum-sucking farm boy!" he bellowed.

Clancy was taken aback. "What?"

"None of us will have anything to do with you, you murderer!" Jack continued.

Clancy caught on and pushed his chair away. "I murder no one!" he answered.

Jack glared at Clancy. "And what about those guards who were blasted to bits last night? The ones who were guarding Willy Woods's girlfriend!"

"I had nothing to do with that!"

"I suppose they just blew up themselves?"

"I told you . . . I murder no one!"

Jack raised a massive left hand. "I told you to leave us alone. We'll not be hired by your kind."

He let his fist go. It connected with Thomas Clancy's chin. The rotund Irishman went tumbling across the floor.

Buddha slowly stood at the table. "And the next time you try to bribe us, Mr. Clancy, you'll be leaving with a lot worse wound than the one you just got."

Clancy stood and rubbed his chin. He flashed a clandestine wink at the Marauders, and then, tail apparently tucked between his legs, left the pub.

The Marauders sat back down at the table. Woods's two men left the inn for a moment. A few minutes later William Woods entered. He walked over to the Marauders, standing, scarecrowlike, above their table.

"So Clancy was indeed after you?" he said.

"Why wouldn't he be?" Mamudi asked.

"And you just stuffed him off?"

"We agreed on a deal last night, didn't we?" Jack replied.

"That we did," Woods said, rubbing his cleft chin with a callused right hand. "And when you're finished with your breakfast, I'll expect you to start earning your money. Meet me over at the house when you're done."

The spindly man walked out of the inn. The Marauders continued their breakfast.

"We're sitting on a powder keg," Kinski said with a sigh.

"One with several short fuses involved," Buddha added.

"We'll do all right," Jack said. "We just have to be careful."

"It's going to be tricky," Mamudi said. "We don't have any backup support."

"I'm hoping for a little at the waterfront from Shatterhand," Jack revealed.

"That still might not be enough," Kinski said.

Mamudi leaned back in his chair. "As water has no constant shape, battle has no constant form. He who is able to adapt to an opponent's action will be victorious and can be called a master . . . Sun Tzu."

"Who the hell was he?" Buddha asked.

"A Chinese militarist," Mamudi replied. "He lived twenty-five hundred years ago."

"He never saw what an automatic weapon can do," Kinski muttered with a smirk.

"No, but he was on to something." Jack grinned. "What we're going to do is beat these boys at their own game."

In the corner of the bar, a thin old man with a long white beard and frizzy, auburn hair began to cackle. The waitress appeared at the Marauders' table to gather up their dishes.

"Who's that?" Jack asked.

"The old man?" the waitress asked.

"The one with the wild eyes and the harmonica smile," Jack answered.

The waitress picked up their plates. "That's Addled Andrew, a real character. He's been here since before my mom's time. He's harmless. Has the brain of a burro but the memory of an elephant."

Addled Andrew continued to stare at the Marauders and giggle in their direction.

Jack turned to the waitress. "What does he do?"

She shrugged. "For as long as I can remember, he palled around with the late Mr. McGuire, the man who worked the lighthouse. Since McGuire's death, I haven't a clue as to how he spends his time. Mostly, these days, he just sits in that chair in the corner and watches things. He doesn't speak much. He just watches."

Jack nodded as the waitress walked away. He caught her by her elbow. "See if he'd like to join us for . . . an early-morning drink."

Jack watched the plump waitress waddle over to Andrew's table. She whispered something to him. The old man nodded and, amazingly spry, leapt out of his chair and hobbled over to the Marauders' spot. He slid a chair beneath him.

"Hiya, boys," he said, cackling.

"Andrew"—Jack nodded—"these are my friends Buddha, Kinski, and Mamudi. They call me Crazy Jack."

"They call me Addled Andrew," the old man said with a wink, "but I'm sure you're just as crazy as I am addled."

"Come again?" Jack said.

The wizened old man stifled a loud laugh. "Oh, I know what you boys are up to."

"And what's that?" Buddha asked.

"You're out to destroy both the Clancy gang and the Woods clan."

The Marauders exchanged panicked glances.

Andrew waved a bony hand in their direction. "Oh, don't worry about my knowing that. Nobody believes anything I say. They think I'm too old and too feeble to have a rational mind."

"Who said we were worried?" Kinski asked.

"Well, just look at your eyeballs, sonny," Andrew said. "You have panic written all around them. If it's any consolation, I don't really give a damn what you do to the bastards. They've held this town in check since before the First World War, which, by the way, I fought in proudly."

"That would make you . . . ," Mamudi began.

"Beats me." Andrew shrugged. "I stopped keeping count after my ninetieth birthday, and I don't know how many years ago that was. The last big war came and time came to a stop. I spotted you four from the first minute you rode into town.

"You're military men, all right, top-notch. And you know what you're doing too. You're not as casual as you crack yourselves up to be."

"And how do you figure that?" Jack asked, mildly amuzed and more than slightly worried.

The old man didn't respond. "I believe you ordered me a drink."

"It's coming," Jack answered.

"My whistle has to be whetted before I start singing," old Andrew said.

A moment later the barmaid placed a lager in front of the skeletal, bearded man. He downed it in less than ten gulps. Crazy Jack was impressed.

"You handle your liquor well," he commented.

"Aye," the old man said. "I inherited that from my father and his father afore him."

He put his empty mug down and stared at the ceiling, motioning toward the Marauders. "In the name of dear St. Patrick, this brings a loving prayer. May you forever be within God's tender love and care. May your hearts be filled with happiness, your homes be filled with laughter. And may the Holy Trinity bless your life forever after."

"Thanks," Mamudi said. "I think—"

"Oh, that was a *real* blessing," Andrew said. "My laddy taught it to me, and his daddy afore him."

"But to get back to what you were talking about . . . ," Jack said.

"Ah, yes." Addled Andrew grinned, his harmonica smile showing, with every other tooth missing. "Well, you see, boys, I was a soldier in the War to End All Wars. World War I. I fought to save my land from the Huns, ye see. And then I fought in World War II. That was supposed to be the Big One. I fought again, to save my land from the Nazi hordes.

"I have a box filled with medals in my wee room to prove it too. I'll show it to ye all sometime."

"I'm sure you were a wonderful soldier," Buddha replied, nodding his round head.

"That I was, Chinaman," Andrew replied. "I like to think that I *still* am. But after a few wars you tend to *hate* what you're doing out there. You tend to notice the blood more and the faces of the dying a lot less. Your mind goes a little numb, if you know what I mean. And do you know what the strangest thing about fighting was?"

Kinski ran a hand through his perfect coif. "I give up."

"Well, you go away to war to save your land and what do you return to? I'll tell you what. You return to a homeland that, even in peacetime, is determined to slug it out; brother out to kill brother just because of what Bible he reads.

"Now, I've never been an overly religious person. One Bible is as good as the other in my eyes. I mean, if you want to see the Lord, whatever Lord you may ascribe to, just go outside and watch the flowers grow, or hear the birds sing, or see the bees a-buzzin' over the flowers that grow and then die and then grow again. That's my religion, gents. That's where *my* Lord is. He's everywhere around us in everything that grows and breathes and lives."

"In some lands you would be called a prophet," Mamudi said, smiling, really liking the old man.

"Aye, in some lands I might be called that," Andrew replied with a nod, "but not here. Hereabouts, everything is black or white, green or orange. There are no middlin' shades. And so I retreated. I kept to myself.

"After World War II, I came back a discouraged, faithless man, I'll admit that. But then I found Old McGuire. He was just a man who loved the sea—couldn't swim a stroke, though. Amazing thing. He could live in that light-house and watch the ships go in and out. But he couldn't swim a stroke.

"I tell ya, though, he could tell when a storm was a-comin' two days before it hit. He could see how the moon affected the tides. He could *sense* when a day would be cloudy or bright. He was an amazing man.

"We just seemed to gravitate to each other. One old war-horse to a slightly younger one. We had the greatest friendship, we did. We weathered many a storm, both natural and political, we did. And our friendship never faltered.

"And when they came—the Woods thugs, I mean—nobody lifted a hand to help him. Not the Clancys. Not his friends. No one. No one but me. They beat me senseless, they did. Addled my brain, so it's supposed."

Andrew stared at the men, a remarkable clarity blazing through his pale gray eyes. "They *slaughtered* him, they did. They made him watch his daughter, Molly, be taken. And then they tortured him. First they put out his eyes. The eyes that had, for years, gazed out upon the sea.

"And then they punished his hands. The hands that had, for just as many years, turned on the mighty light in the lighthouse and guided the ships either to or from the crashing waves and rocks.

"They broke his legs and then riddled his poor, broken body with bullets. And that my boyos, was what Old McGuire got for being a *real* man. An *Irishman*. A man who loved the earth and sky and sea around him and didn't give a good goddamn about what flag flew above the town hall. He loved the *land*, ya see."

Jack motioned the waitress to give Andrew another drink. She placed another mug before him. Andrew stared at it. "Him and me, ya see, always felt that our land was what was most important. It was *Ireland*, whether it 'twas in two or three or four or sixteen pieces. Nobody could deny us our heritage. It was *ours*. But *now*? Now everything is all bollixed up."

He guzzled his grog and gazed up at the ceiling. "Have

you ever been to Ireland, with its rolling hills so green? Sure'n it's the fairest land that ever has been seen. And those green hills of Ireland may be very far away . . . but they're close to every Irish heart, no matter what the day."

Andrew allowed his chin to slope down to his chest. "It's a terrible world we live in, boyos," he muttered.

He rallied himself. "But I have to tell you, as a decorated veteran, I know what you're up to. I talked to dear Mrs. McGuire this morning. She told me how you freed her precious daughter. That's the mark of true warriors, I tell ya.

"And I won't spill a word of it to the enemy."

"And who do you think is the enemy?" Jack asked.

"Well, just look around ye," Andrew answered. "Just about every complacent soul in this town is your enemy. The trouble with most people hereabouts is that they've forgotten what country they belong to! Do ye think I could get behind any one political claque? That would be suicide. Nobody hereabouts cares about Ireland. All they care about is their own arses. And I'm sick and tired of that. I've lived too long and I've cared too much to even consider that way of thinking."

"And what do you care about?" Crazy Jack asked.

"I care about us surviving. No matter what creed, I want Ireland, as a nation, to survive."

"And how do we figure into that, in your way of thinking?" Jack asked.

"Well, I'll tell ya." Andrew nodded semi-drunkenly. "I figure it'll take an outside force to unite us all. It'll take a force from out there to bring us all together against the Federated States of Europe. I figure you boyos have been sent up here to shake things up. And I'm all behind ye. But I'll tell ye what. If you're trying to infiltrate the docks at Londonderry, yer all wrong. The FSE thugs will wipe any of your friends out."

The old man nodded sagely. "See, the thing is, because people consider me a fool, they have a tendency to loosen up their tongues around me. Have conversations they shouldn't. But since they figure I don't know what they're saying, they chatter on like bloody magpies.

"I've heard about this wonderful shipment of guns coming in from the sea. Both families want them, the Clancys and the Woodses. What neither one of them knows is that the Federated sons of bitches are dangling those guns in front of them like a carrot. Each of them think the Federated scum is behind them exclusively."

The old man emitted a wheezing laugh. "You got to hand it to the Federated boys. They *are* rotten, but they are rotten in a very clever way. So, to my way of thinking, you want to get your hands on the guns as well. Well, I know for a personal fact that the people who are runnin' those guns are very well armed. There are a lot of them too. Those black market fellows are cutthroats. They probably already have a few men waiting for the ship. If you fellas try to hunker down at the dock, they'll slaughter you."

"And you have a better suggestion?" Jack asked.

"Sure I do." Andrew nodded. "But you'll have to trust me on this one. There are a lot of old dockworkers who will listen to me instead of the FSE or the bastards who are bringing in the guns, if ye know what I mean."

"I do, sir," Jack answered. "And if these old friends of yours will help us up here, we'll do everything we can to protect their lives."

Andrew cackled. "It's a kind thought, that, but it's not necessary. Old men aren't considered much of a threat. Besides, we all were ready to kick some heini, anyway. We were just biding our time. I can take Old McGuire's car, since he'll not have much cause for usin' it today, and take a lovely drive out to visit my old seamen friends this afternoon. 'Tis a lovely day for a drive, I think."

The old man stared at the Marauders. "So you trust me, then?"

Jack shook his head from side to side, a grin playing across his face. "It doesn't look like we have a choice."

"Crazy Jack," Andrew replied, "in truth, you don't. You either trust me or you kill me. As a corpse, I'm no good to you; as an ally, well, you could do a lot worse."

"And we have at times." Mamudi smiled.

"So," Andrew said, "you do what you have to do here in town. I'll have my boys keep an eye on the Londonderry docks. If you made plans to have any men down there, yank them the hell out before it's too late. If you can't retrieve them, let me know and I'll have some of the old-timers play mother hen to 'em down at the docks."

The old man staggered out of his chair in an exaggerated manner. "Oh," he whispered, "and don't you be worrying about Mrs. McGuire talking you up as heroes. I had a stern conversation with her this morning."

He straightened himself and, making sure everyone was watching, went into his crazy act. "And now, me buckos, I'll be a-goin'," he said loudly.

He leaned down over Jack's head and in a whisper said, "If you need me, I'll either be here or at the lighthouse. I'm a squatter there these days, with Old McGuire gone."

Jack nodded. Addled Andrew walked, on a lopsided angle, toward his place in the corner of the pub, reciting loudly, in a slurred voice, "Good times, good friends, good health to you. And the luck of the Irish in all that you do."

The Marauders watched the old man fall asleep at his table.

"You realize that our cover has been blown," Buddha whispered.

"Not necessarily," Jack surmised. "But it is pretty weird to think that the only person to figure out who we are and what we're doing is the village's official loony. . . ."

"Who turns out to be the sanest man in the village," Mamudi pointed out.

"Well, if the old man doesn't talk," Kinski said, "we've gained three things."

"And what are those?" Buddha asked.

"We've gained an ally, a small army of old dock-workers, and an early-morning drinking buddy," Kinski replied.

Buddha began to clean his glasses with a napkin. "Go ahead, make jokes. We're losing control of the situation here."

Jack sighed in Buddha's direction. "Don't kid yourself. We never *had* control of the situation. When you jump into a whirlpool, you just go with the flow."

Mamudi nodded. "A sage thought. Where did you come across that?"

Jack pondered that. "I dunno. I think it might have been traffic school."

FOURTEEN

Givens, Crane, and Flynn were young and pretty green. All in their mid-twenties, they had joined the British Navy less than a year ago, when good King Shatterhand rose to the throne, aided by the elite team of American mercenaries called the Marauders.

They had never met three of the Yanks in person, but they had seen them all at the coronation ceremony.

For the first time since the last war, they felt a pride in their country.

They had been but teenagers during that war. They didn't fully comprehend who or what the Federated States of Europe represented. To their young way of thinking, the FSE was just a group of people who got the underground running on time again and restored electricity.

Now that they realized that the Federated States of Europe was nothing more than a nouveau Nazi party, they wanted to fight to the death to keep it from reentering England.

And so now they sat, a mile offshore in Londonderry, a small radio in their minuscule launch, monitoring all ship-to-shore communications.

They had been there but a day, and already the cold, dank air was insinuating itself into their bodies, chilling them to the bone.

Mamudi had taught them SEAL tactics: sea, air, and land guerrilla stuff. That had bolstered their spirits. They were learning what amounted to the spy business. Stuff that JFK had put into action back in 1962. But learning that kind of fighting and actually going out on your first mission were two different things.

Givens, Flynn, and Crane sat, their faces blackened to fit in with the dark sea, their boat camouflaged as well.

Flynn scanned the frequencies on the radio, his headset clamped over his ears.

His two fellow seamen searched the sea with bleary eyes, rifles in hand.

Flynn had gotten used to the constant static. It was dulling his concentration. Couldn't allow that, he reasoned. Mamudi had taught them adrenaline was the key. Adrenaline and tunnel vision. There was only the mission. There was no world outside the mission.

The static fluctuated. Words began to form. Flynn's eyes lit up. A heavily accented voice. "Black Dog One to Black Dog Two. Black Dog One to Black Dog Two. Do you read me? Over."

"Black Dog Two. Affirmative. Over."

An Irish voice, that last one.

Flynn strained his ears. The voices were distinct but faint, half buried under an undulating wave of static. ". . . arriving at oh six hundred . . . morrow . . . over . . ."

". . . transport . . . ready . . . oh six hundred . . . over . . ."

". . . will need protection to . . . get to market . . . over . . ."

". . . affirmative . . . barter for best prices . . . over . . ."

The voices faded. The static returned. Flynn put the radio down. "Let's head for shore," he said. "The shipment's arriving tomorrow morning."

He fished inside his pocket for a piece of paper. "Here's the local number we're to call."

His two comrades oared the small boat back to Londonderry. The entire wharf area was enshrouded by fog. Somewhere up above, the sun was shining, but it wasn't strong enough to slice through the thick mist surrounding this seaside town.

Flynn was glad of that. They shouldn't have too much trouble getting to shore and heading for a phone in the shadows afforded by the fog and the various fishing and freight gear scattered along the docks.

He smiled to himself. He had survived his first mission. Not only that, he had succeeded in his first mission.

The three men reached shore and, after removing the black soot from their faces, scrambled onto the docks.

They padded silently down to a phone booth in a deserted area of the dock. Crane and Givens stood guard as Flynn slid into the booth, producing a few coins and jamming them into the phone. He began to dial the number.

He heard the noise before he felt the phone booth explode. His eyes fluttered. Glass slivers tore into his face. He felt something weird about his body.

He had lost control of it.

There was a strange sense of warmth reaching out from his stomach.

Slithering up his spine.

Trickling down toward his ankles.

This wasn't happening, Flynn tried to tell himself. He saw something gushing forward onto the ground outside the phone booth.

Blood.

His blood.

The slivers of glass made his face tingle in pain. Something was wrong with his right eye. He could see nothing out of it. It was gone.

His right hand was still poised in the air, holding a phone receiver that had fallen to the ground a long second ago.

He tried to spin around but he knew he couldn't. A second round nearly took off his upraised right arm.

His head pitched forward and shattered what glass remained in the phone booth. He had time to see Givens and Crane bringing their rifles halfway up to waist level before they, too, were hit.

Two men emerged from the fog, carrying USAS 12-gauge machine guns larger and heavier than the M16s his buddies carried. The two assassins squeezed off round after round from hip level, cruel smiles playing across their faces.

They weren't out just to murder the three boys, they were out to maim them.

Flynn's consciousness faded as he saw his two buddies whirl around and around under the impact of the 12-gauge slugs. He saw them hit the ground.

He saw one of the men approach the phone booth and raise the barrel of the semi-automatic toward Flynn's head.

Then Flynn saw no more.

The two assassins stood over the mangled bodies. One of them noticed a scrap of paper in Flynn's hand. "What do we have here?" he asked his friend.

"Looks like one of our little buggers was about to contact somebody, eh?"

"And he's left us the phone number. Very kind lads, they were."

"Nobody's going to hijack these goods," the second man said, kicking the bodies of Crane and Givens. "Not the FSE, not the Brits, and certainly not you little assholes. Welcome to the world of capitalism."

The first man bent over to retrieve the paper from Flynn's bloodied hand. As he did so, the rear portion of his skull exploded. The man pitched forward onto the ground, heaving one last sigh.

The second man spun around, raising his 12-gauge machine gun. He heard a strange crack-crack-cracking. Three slugs tore through his neck.

He flew backward, his body slamming flat at the feet of Givens and Crane.

Out of the mist stepped Addled Andrew, a well-oiled M-1 rifle in his hands, a souvenir of the Second World War. "Lousy bastards," the old man said, hobbling toward the three slain young boys and the two assassins.

A group of shadowy figures emerged from the fog behind him. Andrew turned to them. "O'Neill, Evans, Fredericks," he said, motioning to the three mangled boys. "Would you be so kind as to take these three heroes away? You have tarp?"

"We do," a chunky man replied.

"Give them a nice burial at sea. They would have liked that, being Navy men and all."

Three of Andrew's friends gently lifted the boys' bodies onto a flat cart and wheeled them off into the mist.

"What about these two?" a guant man asked.

A cold breeze jutted in off the swirling sea, causing Andrew's beard to ripple and his eyes to tear.

He stared at the assassins. "Take their highfalutin guns and save them. As for the rest of 'em, let the fish have them. Bastards. Cowardly, money-grubbing bastards."

Andrew bent over and retrieved a blood-soaked shard of paper. He crumpled up the phone number and tossed it into the sea. Wiping a tear from his eye, he surveyed the dock.

"You might as well scrub the place down, just in case our pair of slugs have any curious friends who might come a-callin'."

A thin dockworker nodded in silence.

"Should we be doing anything else?" he asked.

"No, just keep a watchful eye on things here, gentlemen," Andrew said with a sigh.

The thin man nodded again. "How's the arthritis, Andrew?"

"It just about cripples me," Andrew said. "The damp does me no good at my age, I'll tell you that. How's the wife?"

"Ornery as ever."

"Good to hear," Andrew said. "It's nice to know that some things don't change."

"It's nice to have you back around, Andrew," the thin man said.

The old man slung his World War II rifle over his shoulder and hobbled toward a '56 kelly-green Plymouth. "Just don't tell anybody I'm in full possession of my senses," Andrew said. "I'd hate to sully my reputation."

Addled Andrew eased himself gingerly into the car and drove off toward Feirgall and the sunlight.

Behind him, enshrouded by mist, the dockworkers wrapped three young boys in canvas bags, loaded them onto a small tugboat, and sailed them off to another world.

FIFTEEN

The Marauders sat in William Woods's living room, Willy Woods, his legs bandaged, seething at them from the side. William Woods put his reedlike legs into marching mode, pacing back and forth across the room.

"I think," he said, "it's time we put the fear of God into the Clancys."

The Marauders said nothing.

"Clancy owns property, a lot of it, mostly farmland," Woods said. "About two miles out of town is a large barn. In the past, Clancy has stored his weaponry there. It's heavily guarded. Fortified, probably.

"Young Willy, over there, tried to storm it once and wound up getting a bullet in his behind."

"You want us to take it out?" Jack asked.

"Tit for tat," Woods said. "The Clancys stole the McGuire girl out from under our noses. They butchered our guards. I want blood for blood. By the time you boys are through, I want the fields to run red with Clancy blood.

"Plus, with most of their arms stockpile out of the way, they'll have a slim chance of getting to the black market shipment before we do."

"Excellent plan," Jack said, humoring the old codger. "Just one thing. You expect us to storm the place in broad daylight?"

"They'll never expect *that*!" Woods enthused.

Mamudi nodded. "No, they wouldn't, and with good reason. Militarily speaking, such an assault would be suicide."

"A real cowboy job," Kinski said.

"You said you were professionals," Woods countered.

"*Live* professionals," Buddha said.

"Yellow chink," Willy Woods muttered.

Buddha faced the elder Woods. "For the record, I'm of Mongol ancestry. And also for the record, if that numb-nutted son of yours doesn't keep his mouth shut, I'll send him into low orbit."

"Willy," Woods said casually, "shut your yob."

Willy lapsed into sullen silence.

"So, will you do it?" Woods asked.

"We'll need time to prepare," Jack said.

Woods glanced at a grandfather clock in the corner. "You have three hours."

Mamudi shook his head from side to side. "So much for tactics."

"Tactics?" Woods fumed. "Who needs *tactics*! What tactics did it take to butcher my men last night?"

"You'd be surprised," Kinski said.

"Look," Woods said, "if it's men you need, support, I'll give you two dozen of my best! How's that?"

"Negative," Buddha replied. "We're a four-man unit. We work best on our own. Your men would just slow us down."

"All right," Woods said. "So, what will you do?"

Jack shrugged. "Use C-4 probably. Rig up some claymores around the barn to stop anyone who tries to pursue us."

Woods's eyes sparkled. "C-4, that's an explosive, isn't it?"

"Plastique," Buddha said.

"I like the sound of that. Sounds powerful. And the claymores?"

"Land mines," Kinski said. "Loaded with plastique. They spray pieces of metal for yards."

"This is going to be a grand day," Woods said. "We'll take out the barn and those two little weasles as well."

"What weasels?" Kinski asked.

"Tommy and Jack Clancy. Old Man Clancy's sons. They operate the barn, the sniveling thugs. Imagine how

Old Man Clancy will feel hearing that his sons have been blown sky-high. I love it! I love it! Oh, boys, wait until the FSE hears of this. It will be a glorious day. Simply glorious."

Jack got to his feet. "If there's nothing else?"

"No, no," Woods said, his body now fully animated. "Go about your business. Come back to me and let me know how successful you've been. I have complete faith in you men. Complete and utter faith. Remember, I want blood to flow . . . lots of it."

Buddha, Kinski, and Mamudi stood and shambled off after Jack toward the front door.

"Remember *The Twilight Zone*?" Jack whispered.

"Great show, lousy life-style," Kinski rejoined.

The men left the house and walked toward their jeep. "If we take out that barn, *and* the Clancy kids, we're going to be hip-deep in bad shit," Kinski said.

"I know that," Jack said.

"It's one thing to play two sides against each other for a mission," Buddha said. "But to ambush a group of dim-witted plowboys . . ."

"Who would kill you if they had the chance," Mamudi said.

"Granted," Buddha replied.

"But from a military viewpoint," Mamudi said, "I agree with you. If we do accomplish this task, then the Clancys will be very upset with us and will no longer allow us into their trust. If we do *not* accomplish the mission, then we will be seen as frauds by the Woods group."

"I love logic," Kinski said. "So, basically what you're saying is, we're hip-deep in bad shit."

"In a manner of speaking," Mamudi said.

"That's *my* manner of speaking," Kinski said, bristling. "And I just said that two minutes ago."

Jack cranked up the engine and sent the jeep speeding toward the pub. "I don't see this as a big problem." He shrugged.

"Why not?" Buddha replied.

Jack shrugged. "Three of us will rig the explosives while one of us goes ahead acting as point. We tip off the

Clancys as to what's going to go down. Tell them we have
to pull it off or else we'll be out of Woods's favor, and
since Clancy thinks we're double-crossing Woods and spying for the Clancys, he'll go for it. He'll get his kids out of
there and whatever arms he wants to salvage and we'll
move in.

"We blow the hell out of the barn, give Woods a real
fireworks display, let Clancy off the hook, and then get set
for round two. Let the two of them kill each other, I'm not
wasting my bullets. By tomorrow the two families will be
like cats on a hot plate, not knowing what the hell is going
down."

Mamudi grinned. "The superior warrior causes the
enemy to not know where to defend."

Jack sighed. "That Chinese strategist again?"

Mamudi shook his head. "Traffic school."

SIXTEEN

The Marauders left the Clancy farmhouse, the barrel-chested patriarch trailing behind. Thomas Clancy seemed positively radiant.

"I'm happy to have you fellows on *my* side," Thomas Clancy said.

"Just have the barn cleared out within the hour," Crazy Jack advised.

"And then you can torch her," Clancy replied.

"Oh, we'll do more than torch her," Jack stated.

"Now we have to prepare ourselves," Buddha said, climbing into the awaiting jeep.

"If you need any explosives," Thomas Clancy offered, "we have plenty of dynamite."

"We'll save it until we really need it," Kinski replied.

"Well, whenever you do, it'll be in that shed over there," Thomas replied. "We used to use it for a henhouse, but since the last war, the chickens haven't been right. They have boils and blisters and the egg yolks are blood-red. We killed them all. Burned them. Couldn't eat the meat. Didn't want to take the chance. We're all mostly vegetarians now. I guess you would understand that, Yank. I remember reading about California before the war. A lot of health nuts out there. Never ate meat."

"Never been there," Crazy Jack said, climbing behind the wheel of the jeep. "I was always a steak-and-fries man myself."

"Those were the days." Thomas Clancy sighed. "Those were the days."

The Marauders returned to the inn and made their way up to their rooms. Once inside, they produced their satchels of plastique and rigged up a dozen massive bombs with time-delayed fuses.

They worked in silence.

"You know what I think?" Kinski finally said.

"Uh-uh," Jack replied.

"I don't think Woods quite trusts us."

Jack nodded. "I wouldn't be surprised."

"So," Buddha said from behind his shooter's glasses, "what do we do if he sends men to make sure we slaughter the Clancys?"

"Don't know," Jack replied, working on the bombs.

Mamudi stopped his bomb making for a moment and changed eyes, popping in a nifty orb with an exclamation point on its iris. "He will win who is prepared and waits for the unprepared enemy."

Buddha sighed. "You're not the only one who has read Sun Tzu."

Mamudi attempted to blink. The new eye was too dry. He dabbed some solution into his empty eye socket and replaced the glass orb. "What I'm trying to say...," he began.

"Is that if any of Woods's men show up, they do so at their own risk," Kinski said with a nod. "We *knew* that."

Jack toyed with his bomb. "You know, Freddie," he said, glancing at Mamudi. "You've taken a decidedly religious turn since Tom Bee died."

Mamudi shrugged. "He rekindled my faith, that's true," he admitted.

"And what about those six girls in London?" Buddha chuckled, his massive belly shaking beneath his shirt.

Mamudi smiled slyly. "Also part of my religious beliefs."

Kinski produced a comb and ran it through his well-laminated hair. "This is the only guy in the world who thinks screwing is a religious experience."

"Oh, I dunno," Crazy Jack said. "I always thought it was a better high than most church services."

The four men relaxed in the spirit of their friendship and continued fashioning their bombs.

Three hours later the Marauders went through the motions of zigzagging through the open fields sprawling outside Clancy's barn.

"This is insane," Kinski groused.

"If you have to play the game, you have to play it well," Mamudi, his partner in the mission, whispered.

"Not that Chinese guy again!" Kinski moaned.

"No," Mamudi whispered. "Double Jeopardy. I used to watch it on R and R."

Jack and Buddha rolled up to the rear of the building, placing three plastique boomers against the rear wall.

"This should give the building a lift," Jack said.

Buddha nodded. "You know that we have company, don't you?"

Jack nodded. "Six men on the ridge to our left. Automatic weapons. Two beaten-down cars."

"Woods's men?"

"Sure as hell ain't Clancy's."

"What'll we do?"

"React," Jack said. "We'll wait and see if they make a first move. If they do, we'll make it their *last*."

The two men scrambled back toward their jeep, tucked securely off the road behind the barn. Jack jumped into the back of the jeep where his faithful RPG-2 rocket launcher awaited him.

Within seconds they were joined by the other two Marauders. "We have a few guardian angels here," Kinski hissed breathlessly.

"Let's see what their move is," Jack whispered.

The barn stood serene.

"Should be sky-high soon," Kinski whispered.

Suddenly the barn began to blow in a big way. An immense curlicue of smoke and flame roared up into the afternoon sky, its smoke columns slithering higher and higher. Planks of the building executed turn after turn, trying to reach the sun, before their efforts frittered away, sending the wooden shards tumbling to the ground.

Another blast shattered the quiet of the countryside.

And another.

And another.

What was once a barn "filled" with ammo and supplies erupted into a Mt. Vesuvius of flame and smoke.

The earth rumbled.

Again and again the charges blew, sending orange and white-hot flame, and columns of smoke everywhere.

Within minutes the barn site was reduced to nothing more than a large crater.

"They'll be wondering why there's no bloody bodies emerging," Jack theorized.

"They'll want a firefight," Mamudi said.

"If they do, we'll give them one," Jack answered.

The half dozen men sent by Woods to supervise the supposed slaughter dived into their two battered cars, which, from Jack's viewpoint, looked like '63 Chevy Impalas. The two cars rumbled toward the crater.

"Well," Jack said with a sigh, "since we've pulled this off successfully and Woods wants blood . . ."

"Let's give him some," Kinski rejoined.

Jack manned the rocket launcher.

He crouched above it, fondling it in an almost loving way. "Come on, darling," he cooed.

He squeezed off two 40-mm rounds at the two cars.

"Please, baby," he coaxed.

The four Marauders watched the cars rumble forward, three men in each.

The first car rounded a curve in the dirt road, headed toward where the barn once was.

Without warning, the lead car ignited.

In a blink of an eye, the car was reduced to a massive fireball of heat and steel.

Four tires went into orbit.

A massive hole in the earth remained where the car had once hugged the road.

The second car, noting the instant disappearance of the first, made a subtle move to avoid the hole in the earth.

Before the driver had a chance to maneuver the car around the crater, it, too, disappeared.

A zing.

A screech.

The sound of metal giving way.

The stench of death.

The second car went up in a fireball and a shriek of surprise.

The Marauders watched as the last vestiges of the car tumbled down to the dank, damp earth.

Smoke was everywhere.

"Well," Jack said, still clutching his RPG-2, "I guess we gave Woods the blood and the body count he wanted."

Buddha nodded. "Maybe."

Mamudi turned to Jack. "Exactly how do you plan on explaining all this carnage?"

Jack eased himself away from the weapon. "Shit, Freddie. The Clancys came out of the fiery barn, weapons held high. They shot at anything that came at them."

"And," Kinski added, "unfortunately it was Woods's men."

"You got it," Jack said, sliding behind the wheel. "Now, let's get home."

En route back to the town, the Marauders slowed down to pick up an old, spindly hitchhiker.

It was Addled Andrew.

And he had great tales to tell.

SEVENTEEN

The Marauders swung old Addled Andrew onto the back of their jeep.

"What the hell are you doing out here?" Crazy Jack asked.

"I'm out here to save your butts." Andrew nodded, the wind whistling through his beard.

"I was afraid of this." Kinski sighed, allowing the afternoon breeze to buffet his well-moussed forehead. "You realize that you can blow our cover?"

"Your cover came close to being blown already." The old man sat, spitting over the side of the jeep.

"What do you mean?" Jack asked.

"The men you sent to Londonderry?" Andrew began.

"What about them?" Jack snapped.

"Dead'r than doornails, slaughtered in the worst way," Andrew answered. "'Twas a terrible, bloody sight."

"Who did it?" Buddha said, trying to keep his anger from boiling over.

"Black marketeers," Andrew replied. "Don't worry, I took them out. And I provided the kind of military funeral for the three lads that you would have welcomed."

"I bless you for that," Mamudi said.

"I don't need *your* goddamn blessing," Andrew groused. "What I want is a way to wreak revenge. The average people have been shell-shocked around here for many a year . . . it's time to bring all this crap to a stop. When I die, I want to die in a peaceful place, and I don't want any two sides punching each other's noses in over

113

what graveyard I'm allowed to get tossed into."

"I'm with you there, Andrew," Jack said.

"That's all well and good to say, but I want to see words put into action."

"Give us a chance, Andrew," Buddha breathed. "We're in a bad way up here."

"And don't I know it." Old Andrew cackled. "I've been in a few hard scrapes myself."

"*You* took out the assassins yourself?" Kinski blurted.

"Aye, that I did." Andrew nodded. "I was fighting in wars that were goin' on before you were a gleam in your papa's eye. But I have to tell ya, I didn't rely totally on your greenies out there. I had some of my old boys up to their tricks and it paid off."

"In what way?" Mamudi asked.

"Well, the way I figure it, you trained your young laddies pretty well . . . but training's one thing. Being dropped into battle is something other. When I met yez yesterday, I phoned a friend at the dock site. They were a-listen' as well as your three brave lads out there. The old duffer picked up the same radio communications as your boyos out in the drink."

"So they died in vain," Jack muttered.

"The hell they did," Addled Andrew said, poking a bony forefinger into the brawny redhead's back. "They died for *freedom,* and there's no way that can be dismissed. They died as *heroes,* you bastard son of a bitch, and don't you ever forget that."

Andrew snuggled into the backseat. "What we all heard was the fact that these guns everyone is crazy about are landing at port tomorrow morning at six A.M. I don't know any more about it but that. I have my old men watching, but you know how old men can be. If I were you boys, I'd be out there before five. I'd be waiting for them guns. I'd be waiting for the ones who slaughtered those three boyos. And if you let me, I'd be honored to stand beside you."

Addled Andrew stroked his beard. "When I was their age, I was just *thinking* about lying about my age in order to get into the war to end all wars."

Andrew stroked his beard once more. "It would be an

honor to shed blood for those lads. I mean, think of their would-be children, and their children's children. I want to blow those bastard black marketeers away, young lads. I'm tired of spending my life sitting on my duff."

Andrew turned to the four men. "If you let me do *that,* I swear I'll never bother you again."

Buddha said, "We won't deny you that, Andrew."

"We're all in agreement on that." Mamudi nodded.

"Great." Andrew smiled. "Then let's head for the pub. There's spirits there I haven't even tried yet."

Mamudi nodded. "There are spirits *we* haven't even called upon yet."

The Four Marauders sat in silence on the way back to the village, remembering the essence of Tom Bee, and the myriad of spirits he had evoked.

EIGHTEEN

Crazy Jack, Mamudi, Buddha Chan, and Kinski made a stop at the Clancy home.

"It's done" was all Jack said before turning away.

"Do you think Woods bought it?" the elder Clancy called.

"I'm sure he will," Jack muttered.

A half hour later Jack stood before William Woods.

"Well?" the skeletal Irishman asked.

"The barn has been taken out," Jack said, seething.

"Casualties?" Woods asked anxiously.

"Quite a few," Jack replied, the Maruaders glaring at Woods from behind him.

"Did they die in pain?" Woods said, licking his chapped lips.

"Oh, I'm sure they did," Jack replied. "And quite a few of the dead were your own men."

Woods's face went ashen. "I . . . I don't understand."

Jack puffed out his chest and reared himself to his full, Olympian height. "Oh, I'm sure you do, William. In this deal, you either trust us or you don't. You sent a half dozen men out there today to make sure we got the job done.

"Well, *we* did . . . but your men got caught up in a fairly intense crossfire."

"My men?" Woods gasped.

"There's not enough left of them to stuff into an American hot-dog bun."

Woods took this all in. "I'm sorry, lads. You have to

understand my position. I find it hard to trust men *without* religion."

"Without a religion similar to yours," Mamudi added.

"Aye." Woods nodded. "I'm sorry if I caused you hardship today."

"Not *us,*" Buddha injected. "Your own soldiers."

Woods seemed to stagger under the assault of words. "I know, I know. It was my *own* that was killed. But," he added, "I don't want you to feel that you were responsible for it."

Jack nodded. "We don't. It was your own stupidity that caused the massacre."

Woods blanched at that.

Jack shrugged his massive shoulders. "But I'm sure that after this, you'll never doubt our loyalty again."

"No, sir, I won't," Woods said.

"You'd better not." Kinski winked. "You're paying us plenty for it."

The Four Marauders turned as one, and marched out of Woods's home.

The spindly man watched them leave in silence.

In the corner of the room, his bandaged son, Willy, sat sprawled across a sofa.

"Is all this worth it, Papa?" he whined.

"Of course it is," the elder Woods snapped.

"But what if it isn't?"

His father spun toward him. "It *has* to be," the elder Woods roared.

Silence.

"But suppose we're being used by—"

"By *whom*?" Woods screamed.

"By the FSE," Willy Woods offered.

"If we *are* being used by the FSE," the elder Woods proclaimed, "then let us be used in the way our forefathers would have wanted. In a way that will benefit our cause."

Willy Woods sulked in the corner. "Our cause this, our cause that. It doesn't make sense anymore. It's not *my* cause. It's not half of the people's cause anymore. Don't you see, Papa? Those causes are long gone. They just don't matter anymore. The whole world has been nearly destroyed, and when Jesus comes a-calling, when Armageddon *does* happen, it's not going to matter very much *what* kind of cross he's carrying. He'll get here all the same."

"Blasphemy!" the elder Woods spat.

"Blasphemy?" Willy chuckled. "*That's* blasphemy, but two different groups shooting each other's hearts out in the name of God isn't?"

"It's a holy war!"

"The hell it is. If things were normal around here, I could have courted Molly McGuire, not kidnapped her. I could have loved her, not raped her."

"You wanted her, and I got her for you," William Woods said angrily.

"Yeah, right," Willy said. "And in the process we killed her father and locked up her mother. I tell you, Papa, I just can't get mad over this crap anymore. Maybe it was the bullets in my leg. Maybe it was seeing our men butchered for no other reason than me playing tough guy. But it doesn't make sense anymore."

"You're a coward," his father said with a sneer. "You get shot up a little bit and you turn yellow."

"No," Willy said. "I got shot up *quite* a bit. When you can't move around, you have a lot of time to think . . . and what I've been thinking lately is that when I'm healed, I'm moving south. I'm leaving this place."

"You'll be murdered down there," William told his boy.

"I don't think so, Papa. I don't care much about what kind of church I go to every week. I just want to go to one that's not got blood on the front steps."

"I'll kill you before you desert this land."

"You just may have to, Papa," Willy said.

The elder Woods strode out of the room.

Willy Woods tried to swing his legs up onto the couch. He couldn't quite make it.

"You don't get it, Pop," he whispered. "We're all dying here . . . and it just doesn't matter."

Willy Woods felt himself sinking into a deep sleep. "It's not Orangemen and Greenmen anymore," he mumbled. "It's Irishmen against *them*. And they're pulling our strings."

He began to nod off. "It's us against the outsiders," he mumbled. "It's *us* . . .," he repeated.

Outside the Woods home, the Marauders slid into their jeep, taking stock of the situation.

They had the guns.

They had the explosives.

They had to take out a convoy on the morrow.

And they also had to bluff the takeout for two employers who dearly wanted the firepower.

They knew they could easily waste the black marketeers. They could snatch the guns.

But where to hide them?

And how to play the Clancys off the Woods in a way that would stymie the FSE?

They had a lot of planning to do, and very little time to do it.

NINETEEN

The black marketeers guided the freighter into the harbor just before dawn.

Mist swirled around them.

They unloaded crate after crate of guns and ammo.

They carefully placed the cargo onto six large, canvas-covered trucks.

They smiled and nodded to each other.

They waved to the freighter as it pulled away.

That's when the first man stepped on the tripwire mine.

A bouncing Betty.

The man screeched as the explosive device whirled before him, slowly detonating, sending shards of metal fragments into his chest as well as into the six men around him.

Several pirates lurched around the flailing, dying men, confused.

They scattered.

Bad move.

From the mist emerged round after round of hot, sputtering, sizzling lead.

A few of the fleeing pirates took the bursts full in the torso. Their bodies tumbled back off the pier into the deep, cold waters of the swirling, churning sea.

The remaining black marketeers ran for the trucks, all to no avail.

One caught a rocket in the spleen.

His body disappeared before the frightened eyes of his comrades.

The black marketeers raised their weapons, Uzis mostly,

lightweight, easy to handle. They had been taken by surprise, true. Half of their number had just fallen prey to an ambush. But there was a fortune to be made here. Money still bought power, even in the post-nuked world. And power brought more power. And what was life about, if not *power*? The pirates trained their weapons on the fog wall before them.

They had no real plan except to wait to spot the flaring muzzles of their attackers' weapons and then spray the area.

Before they could squeeze off a round, the fog wall erupted with tiny eyes of bright orange light.

The slugs tore into the black marketeers, sending their bodies twitching and turning in the predawn mist.

The slugs passed through their sweating flesh and zoomed inside the macadam and wood beneath them.

One pirate made a leap for the driver's seat of the lead convoy truck.

He heard a swishing noise from behind him.

He found himself impaled, at the neck, by a swirling, slashing Chinese fighting knife.

Another ran toward the second truck.

The *bing-bing-bing* of an M16 rang out.

The man staggered back, a third eye of lead suddenly appearing in the middle of his forehead.

He plopped against a wooden pillar.

Twelve pirates remained.

Their cargo and their future fortunes were at stake.

They ran for the six trucks, filled with ammunition and a guarantee of a rich lifetime.

An AK-47 opened up from the skies above.

Six men went down immediately, their insides becoming outsides within seconds.

The six remaining men struggled toward the trucks.

One was shattered by a rocket.

Another stepped on something soft. He heard the roar from beneath his feet. His legs tumbled high in the air above his head.

He couldn't believe it.

It didn't matter.

He dropped, squirming, onto the dock.

Another man ran into the mist, where a group of elderly men, led by Addled Andrew, beat him to a bloody pulp, using nothing more than planks.

He glanced up at the old men.

He had never seen so many angry men in his life. He began to chuckle, the blood spurting from his mouth and dribbling from his ears.

Killed by codgers.

Bullets sang through the air.

Human flesh was pelted from all sides.

Human forms jiggled and jerked.

After a while there was only one black marketeer left. He dived into the front truck.

He revved the engine.

Rip van Winkle appeared from the mist.

The black marketeer gasped.

Rip van Winkle raised a vintage rifle carefully and squeezed off a clear shot.

The driver's head exploded.

Soon all was quiet.

The four Marauders emerged from the fog.

Jack walked up to Addled Andrew. "Nice shot" was all he said.

"I know it, pipsqueak," Andrew said, lowering his World War II weapon.

"Well," Buddha said, "we have the works."

"Now we have to stash them," Kinski rejoined.

"And play the game," Mamudi answered.

Jack turned to Andrew. "Will your friends take a few more chances?"

Andrew nodded. "Hell, this is the first time they've got to do some good in years and years."

"We'll have to move quickly and empty the trucks," Jack said.

"You can store the cargo here," a man named Henneghan said. "Nobody uses the docks much these days."

"And then the trucks and whatever bodies you can salvage have to be moved halfway to town."

"Make it look like a roadside ambush?" Andrew asked.

"That's the ticket," Jack said.

"And then," Kinski added, "barring any hitches, we just sit back and let the Clancys and the Woodses shoot it out. That will put a crimp in the FSE's control of the area."

"Your lips to God's ears," Andrew prayed.

TWENTY

Crazy Jack Keenan appeared just after dawn at the back of the Clancy farm. The barrel-chested patriarch of the family, Thomas Clancy, strode out of the house.

"You're taking a chance coming here," he hissed, "in broad daylight."

Jack's teeth were chattering. The sun would not be able to make an appearance that morning. Rivers of swirling, blue-gray clouds filled the sky. It was cold. It was damp. It was anything but broad daylight.

"I thought you'd be interested in knowing about the arms shipment," he said.

Clancy beamed. "Now *that* I would be."

"It's arriving at noon today," Jack said.

"Londonderry docks?"

"Correct."

The patriarch scratched his thinning hair. "What do you suggest?"

"The way I hear it, the convoy will be heading toward town on the main highway ready to make a deal with the first bidder. Woods already has plans to meet them on the highway at thirteen hundred hours."

"What?"

"Approximately one o'clock this afternoon. Apparently he has some connections with the men at the docks and got word to the freighter."

"The cheating bastard!" Clancy was fuming.

"So if I were you, I'd get my money and the gift of gab ready and set out to meet them a half hour ahead of time.

Once you convince the arms dealers that you're the better man to make the deal, you're safe. If Woods and his men show up at one, even if they want a fight, they'll be out-numbered. Your men will be there. The black marketeers will be there. Plus, there's the element of firepower. You'll have enough guns and ammunition to blow the Woodses and half of this country sky-high."

"I like it," Clancy said. "I like that a lot."

"Or," Jack continued, "if you don't want to deal, just take them by surprise. Steal the guns. By the time Woods gets there, he won't find anything but empty trucks and a whole group of surprised and deceased arms dealers."

"I like that *better*," Clancy said.

"I have to go now," Jack said. "It's almost time for breakfast."

"Thank you, boy," Clancy said, beaming. "You're a fine, freedom-loving man."

Jack grinned. "You'll never know the half of it."

Jack turned and trotted into the rising early-morning damp. Within seconds his massive frame had been enveloped by tendrils of swirling, spiraling mist.

Clancy returned to the house, bellowing. "Where are my sons? Where are my brothers? It's time to *act!*"

The sounds of footsteps echoed around the house. Thomas's brothers, Sean and Ryan, appeared, breathless, as did his sons, Tommy and Jack.

"This will be a memorable day for the Clancy family," Thomas announced.

"Today we will both defeat the Woodses and their supporters and be taken into the protective arms of the Federated States of Europe!"

William Woods was in a bad mood. He hadn't been able to stomach even looking at his son, Willy, for a day. The boy, his legs bandaged, sat in silence on the couch in the living room. Woods wouldn't even help the boy up to the bedroom. Let him crawl, he theorized.

Let the wounds reopen.

Let infection set in.

Let the ungrateful little bastard die. He was no son of

Woods's, that was for sure. He was pro-Papist. In Woods's eyes he was no better than a slug.

He was still staring, disgusted, at his son, when there was a knock at the door.

He ambled over to the front door and swung it open. The Marauders stood there.

"I have no work for you today, boys." Woods sighed. "I'm having some problems here at home, and my sources at the docks haven't contacted me since yesterday."

"Well," Jack said, entering, "*we* have news."

Buddha offered a sly grin. "Something I think you'll like."

"And what might that be?" Woods asked.

"You know the old man at the pub?" Kinski said.

"The one everyone assumes is touched?" Mamudi continued.

"Addled Andrew Harrigan." Woods nodded. "The man's had his head up his ass for so many years, I dismiss him as a doughnut."

"Well, your *doughnut* seems to have quite a few contacts at the Londonderry docks," Jack said.

"Of course he does." Woods shrugged. "The man's been sidling up to the sea since my father's time. So what?"

"So," Jack continued, "what if I told you that *he* heard from one of his dockworker friends that a very large shipment of cargo was arriving in port at . . . *two* this afternoon?"

Woods frowned. "I wouldn't put too much faith in that," he said, shrugging again. "Most of Andrew's friends are almost as crazed as he is. Old men. Heavy drinkers. You have to understand, boys, that the docks haven't been that busy since the last war. Most of those men up in Londonderry just show up every day because there's no place else for them to go. Human ghosts, that's what they are, haunting the place that once gave them a livelihood."

"Well"—Jack nodded—"since you have no use for us today, I suppose we should be off. Take in the sights and all."

"And if our report should be accurate." Mamudi shrugged.

"And if the Clancy family gets hold of the shipment for some strange reason," Buddha added.

"Well," Kinski said with a sigh, "call me crazy, but if I were you, I might want to check it out."

"Go to the docks?" Woods ventured.

"No," Crazy Jack said. "You don't want to tip your hand. If you want to barter with this bunch for the guns, meet them on the road. If you want to *ambush* them and take the guns, surprise them on the road. These men are businessmen, not real fighters."

Woods nodded. "That's good advice there, son. Suppose you meet me here at one? I'll have some of my men gathered, and we'll ride out and just stop those thieving merchants cold."

"Sounds like a plan," Kinski said.

The four men left. William Woods stood in the doorway, watching the quartet march off toward their jeep. "This will be the day," he whispered to himself. "This will be the day that I rid this town of the Clancys and strike a blow for the FSE and the true United Kingdom."

TWENTY-ONE

Thomas Clancy motioned his twenty men out of their trucks. He stood next to his two brothers and two sons, binoculars in his hands. He squinted his eyes, peering through the lenses, a scowl appearing on his face.

He handed the binoculars to his brother, Ryan. "What do you think of that?" he asked softly.

The men stood at the edge of a wooded area a half mile from the road leading to Feirgall. Ryan, adjusting the focus of the binoculars, saw six trucks sitting in the middle of the road.

There were no signs of life or movement.

"Could be a trap," Ryan said, passing the binoculars to brother Sean.

"Doesn't make sense," he said. "The black market boys are a bad lot, but they'd have no call to kill us. For all they know, we're just possible customers."

Thomas Clancy surveyed the scene one more time. "I can't see any guards down there, but I can make out the figure of a driver or two. The drivers aren't moving."

He heaved a deep sigh. "So basically, either the arms dealers are waiting for customers, or planning an attack, or have already met one."

Ryan blinked. "You don't think the Woodses would have—"

"They're capable of anything . . . and there's only one way to find out. Ryan, you and half the men come with me. Sean, stay here with Tommy and Jack and the rest.

Cover our rears. If anything happens to us down here, you know what to do."

"We'll swoop down on 'em with the fierceness of banshees," Sean Clancy said.

Thomas Clancy swung himself behind the wheel of one of his pickup trucks. Ryan did the same in another. Five men piled into the back of each.

The two farm trucks slowly rumbled down the embankment leading toward the roadside.

There was still no movement to be seen from the gun merchants.

The two farm trucks paced each other, easing onto the highway and cautiously puttering toward the lead truck.

"Damn!" Thomas Clancy yelled, pointing toward the first of the six gun dealers' trucks.

The reason the driver inside was not stirring was that the top half of his head had been blown off.

Thomas Clancy sent his farm truck skidding to an abrupt halt. He clambered out of the vehicle, his men in tow.

"Sweet Jesus in heaven," he muttered, walking past the lead truck. The far side of the truck was bullet-riddled in a major way, not small slug holes but large, gaping, jagged ones.

Clancy moved silently to the back of the first truck and untied the canvas. A pile of badly mangled bodies were sprawled in the back.

"There's our arms dealers," Clancy growled.

He motioned for the rest of the men high above the ridge to join him.

Two more farm trucks barreled down the embankment toward the massacre.

"There's more of them back here," Ryan said, undoing the canvas on the second truck.

"And back here," one of Clancy's men called from the third truck.

Clancy's other brother, Sean, pulled up, with the two Clancy sons riding shotgun. "What's happened?"

"Our dealers have been killed, *butchered* being a better

word," Thomas Clancy said, his already mottled face growing the color of raw chopped chuck.

"And the guns?"

"Taken right from beneath our noses."

Ryan walked up to his brother. "It *has* to be the Woodses."

Clancy nodded. "Don't I know it. Well, they've gone too far this time. We had the Federated States' men behind us on this one. The Woodses will pay for this, and they're going to pay *hard*. Let's get back to the farm and do a little planning."

"What about all these bodies?" Ryan asked.

Thomas Clancy leapt behind the wheel of his truck. "Let the birds have them."

He sent his truck roaring back toward his farm.

"It doesn't seem like a very Christian thing to do," Ryan said to no one in particular, "leaving these people out here without proper burial."

"Not to worry," Sean said. "They probably weren't Christians, anyway."

The small convoy of farm trucks sped from the scene, leaving the six shattered arms trucks with its rancid cargo sitting in the middle of the road.

TWENTY-TWO

The four Marauders led the Woodses' convoy of cars and trucks through the damp, dark countryside.

Woods, himself, sat in the second car, grinning happily from behind the wheel. In a few moments he'd have more firepower than he had ever dreamed of.

In a few days he'd be rewarded by the FSE, and after that, he'd *personally* put an end to both the Clancys and all their ilk. He'd end the troubles once and for all.

For a moment he thought dreamily about how Northern Ireland would finally reflect the will of his people.

The jeep in front of his station wagon slowed down. The Marauders gazed down onto the road.

Woods swung his car up to the jeep. "Have the guns arrived as yet?"

Crazy Jack backed away from the ridge. "They have," he said.

"Wonderful," Woods said enthusiastically.

"Maybe," Kinski said.

"It doesn't look right down there," Mamudi added.

"The trucks are just sitting in the middle of the road," Buddha said.

"What?"

Woods scrambled to the edge of the incline. True enough, six canvas-covered vehicles sat listlessly in the center of the highway leading into town.

"What the devil is going on down there?" Woods whispered.

"Beats me," Jack replied. "But whatever it is, it isn't

good. You and your men wait up here, we're going down for a look."

Woods nodded mutely, expecting the worse. "Have a care, boys. It smells like a trap."

"It smells, all right," Jack said. "But what my nostrils are picking up smells more like death."

Jack made a great show of stoically sliding behind the wheel of the jeep. Mamudi, Buddha, and Kinski hardened their jaws and cradled their weapons in the best of Sergeant Rock styles as the jeep sailed down the incline and onto the roadway.

"Do you think he's buying it?" Kinski asked.

"I *know* he's buying it," Jack replied.

The jeep fishtailed onto the road. The Marauders leapt out and, surrounding the convoy, inched up to the backs of the trucks in a very exaggerated style.

They whipped back the canvas covers on the vehicles.

Addled Andrew and his over-the-hill gang had made a good job of placing the bodies and the weaponry in such a manner as to suggest an ambush.

For added reality, they had even shot holes in the canvas coverings once they had removed the weaponry stored there. Jack turned toward the hillside.

He raised a hand to Woods.

Woods, cursing, climbed into his station wagon and motioned his men down the hill.

Within minutes a very angry William Woods was surveying the scene.

"Damn," he muttered over and over again. "Damn. Damn. Damn. We're up the creek now, boys, bereft of paddles."

"You think the Clancys have the guns?" Kinski asked.

"Well, isn't it obvious?" Woods replied. "Look at this carnage. These foreigner assholes didn't know what hit them. Everything they were carrying is gone. I'm surprised those bloody scavengers didn't take these idiots' weapons as well."

"They probably didn't want to hang around too long," Jack said.

"Can you tell when it happened?" Woods asked.

Mamudi approached one of the bodies inside the truck. The blood had already congealed, and rigor mortis was setting in. He had to bluff it. "It's hard to tell because of the damp and cold but, offhand, I'd say within the last two hours or so."

"How did *they* know when the convoy was coming through?" Woods muttered. "My men at the docks have said nothing for over a day. If it wasn't for you boys, I wouldn't even have known about the cargo coming through at all."

Jack nodded sagely. "Well," he said flatly, "it could be just dumb luck."

"I doubt that," Woods said.

"Or maybe the Clancy folks have a man or two at the docks themselves."

"They wouldn't dare attempt that," Woods said. "They'd be flying in the face of the FSE!"

"Well, *you* dared," Kinski retorted. "And as far as the Clancys are concerned, you're an independent outfit. Why shouldn't they try the same?"

Woods nodded. "It *does* make sense, at that, doesn't it?"

Buddha wiped the fog from his shooter's glasses. "And if *their* men surprised *your* men, well, that would explain why you haven't heard a word in twenty-four hours."

Woods's scarecrow face grew granitelike. "Then there's only one thing left for us to do. . . ."

"And what's that?" Jack asked.

"Ride into town, slaughter every last one of them, and get those weapons back!"

"You *could* do that." Mamudi nodded. "But with the Clancys all dead, how would you find the shipment?"

"You're going to have to be clever about this," Kinski said. "Outfox your enemy."

"And how do you propose to do that?" Woods asked.

Jack remained silent. The man was following their lead like a snake to a charmer's tune.

"Well," he said, "why not propose a meeting?"

"I wouldn't want that ilk in my home!" Woods declared.

"Not in your home," Jack said. "The Clancys will never go for that."

"A neutral place," Mamudi offered. "Maybe the pub. Invite them to have dinner with you. Leave their guns at the door. Discuss peace with them."

"I could never do that!" Woods sputtered.

"We're not suggesting you do, for real," Jack said. "Let's see how it plays out. The Clancys have the weaponry, which you both want and need. They're in the power position now. But suppose you concoct a tale: You want to unite the two families, the two sides, put all your religious squabbles behind you. . . . "

"They won't buy it," Woods said.

"Perhaps they will if you tell them that England and its new king want to invade Northern Ireland, conquer it, just to hinder the FSE."

"Now why would I want to fight the king?" Woods said. "Thomas Clancy is no fool. I've been a supporter of the United Kingdom forever."

"But it's not your real king," Jack said, pressing on. "He's a Scot. He doesn't care about your church or your customs. Let's say that all he'd be interested in is screwing the FSE, and to do that, he'll kill *anyone, any* side that tries to stop him."

Woods considered this. "Clancy might buy that . . . if he felt that he was in as much danger as we were. Yes, he just might. It would be like fighting the Nazis when you put it that way."

"And then when the Clancys enter the pub," Jack said, "you nail them. Show your strength. Force them to tell you where the guns are."

Woods was smiling now. "A good piece of strategy, that," he said.

"Of course, you'll have to convince them to come," Jack continued.

"And you'll have to have a few of your men hide weapons inside the pub beforehand," Mamudi said.

"That way," Buddha continued, "all the parties involved

can make a great show of being frisked and leaving their guns at the door."

"And who'll do the frisking?" Woods asked.

"Well, since everyone knows that we are *not* men of religion"—Mamudi smiled slyly—"I think we could be the representatives of common justice here."

Woods began to cackle. It wasn't a pretty sound. "Yes, yes. I like it. I like this very much."

He turned to his car. "All right, then. We'll all return home and then send out a few men to invite the Clancys over."

Woods stopped in mid-step. "I have an idea," he said, beaming. "Why don't *you* four go over to the Clancy house and invite them over? As you said, you're outsiders. Everyone knows that the only reason you're working for me is that I'm paying you cold, hard cash.

"You explain the situation, Jack, with your silver American tongue. Set them all up really nicely now. Make them feel at ease. While you're over there, I'll send a few of my boys over to Barney's. Any suggestions where we should hide the weapons?"

Jack shrugged. "You can tape them under a few tables. Bathroom stalls are good as well. Anyplace your men will have access to and not appear conspicuous. Try to keep the weapons small as well. You don't want to have the problem of trying to raise a shotgun taped to the bottom of the table. You might wind up lifting the whole table and blowing off someone's foot. Plus, it'll give the Clancys time to flee."

"Good advice," Woods said. "Excellent advice. You men are true professionals."

"Oh, we're that, all right," Mamudi said with a grin.

The four Marauders watched Woods and his men drive off toward town.

They faced the six trucks. "What should we do about these guys?"

Jack walked over to the jeep. "Might as well incinerate the bodies."

He picked up his RPG-2 rocket launcher and sent a half

dozen 40-mm rounds into the gas tanks of the truck.

Within moments the road was filled with burning debris and the stench of charred flesh.

The four men left the scene in silence.

Even though their mission was rolling on full tilt, the amount of blood they'd be spilling in a few days time numbed them.

TWENTY-THREE

The Marauders drove up to the entrance of the Clancy farm and were met by a group of hostile men, including brothers Ryan and Sean and gangly sons Tommy and Jack.

"What does the likes of you want here?" Ryan demanded.

"We have a message from Woods," Jack said.

"And what might that be?" Ryan answered.

"It's from Mr. William Woods to Mr. Thomas Clancy," Jack said.

He noted that there were a good dozen men appearing from behind the farmhouse, rifles drawn.

"All right, all right," Ryan muttered. "Drive up to the front of the house and I'll fetch my brother."

The Marauders did as they were told. They pulled the jeep up in front of the house. "Leave your weapons inside the jeep, mercenaries."

Mamudi, Jack, Buddha Chan, and Kinski made a production of disarming themselves. They walked inside the house where a frantic, squat man was pacing.

"We have a message from Woods" was all Jack said.

Both brothers and the two sons had followed the Marauders inside the house. Thomas Clancy shot them a withering look. "Get out of here! I'll talk to these men alone!"

"Do you think it's wise, Dad?" Tommy asked.

"How long have I been running this household?" Thomas snapped.

Clancy's four kinsmen backed out of the house in a

crablike manner, slamming the front door securely behind them.

"What does Woods want?" Clancy said.

"He says he wants a truce," Jack replied.

"A truce? And him with enough weaponry to slaughter every Catholic from here to the southern border?"

Mamudi nodded. "Still, it might be to your advantage to play along."

"And how's that? Woods somehow got to the arms before I did, and now I have the FSE men breathing down my neck. I'll be the laughingstock of Northern Ireland. Worse than that, I'll be totally powerless."

"Consider this," Buddha offered. "If Woods is offering the peace branch, he must have a reason."

"So?" Clancy snapped.

"And perhaps that reason betrays a certain *weakness* on his part," Mamudi continued. "If he has the firepower..."

"Of course he has the firepower," Clancy nearly spat.

"...then his peace offering has to be made out of fear. Perhaps he knows that the Federated States of Europe are backing *your* side and he doesn't want to provoke an altercation that would place him in their bad graces."

"Speak English!" Clancy fumed.

"What he's trying to say," Kinski said, slouching in a chair, "is that maybe Woods wants to suck up to you because he's afraid if he crosses you, he'll have the FSE gnawing on his skinny behind."

"Now why didn't you just say that!" Clancy said to Mamudi.

"I did." Mamudi shrugged.

"Ah, I'm getting sick of foreigners," Clancy muttered. "So what does Woods suggest?"

"A meeting tonight at Barney's Inn," Jack said.

"What time?"

"Let's say seven," Jack answered.

"Great, so I'm just supposed to walk in there and face this cobra?" Clancy muttered.

"No," Jack said. "What you do is send a few men ahead to stash some arms. Small arms. Hide them effectively and swiftly. Woods has agreed that everyone should enter the building unarmed."

"Your suggestion?" Clancy grinned.

"Uh-huh," Jack answered. "We'll be frisking everyone at the door. When Woods begins to wheedle a deal, you surprise him."

"That I will," Clancy said. "I'll blast the scrawny son of a bitch to hell and back, but only after I find where he's hidden the guns."

Jack leaned against a wall. "You haven't told anyone about our *arrangement,* have you?"

"Not a soul," Clancy replied.

"Good." Jack sighed. "Because if any one of your men even suspected, this could all blow up in our faces. Woods wouldn't have us guarding the pub and he could try to pull anything he wanted. If he had a couple of drinks in him and was feeling cocky, FSE or no, he could open up on you as soon as you walked into the place."

Clancy nodded. "I get your drift. You're real guardian angels, you know that, don't you?"

Clancy slapped Jack on the back. "It's nice to find a man who defends *real* principles these days."

Jack nodded. "We'll defend them to the death, Mr. Clancy."

"That's what I like to hear," Clancy said. "Now prepare yourself. I'm going to make a ruckus at the door."

Clancy walked the Marauders to the front door. He swung it open, bellowing, "And you can tell that son of a bitch bastard that if he even *thinks* he can try anything tonight, I will personally put a bullet in his brain."

"Yes, sir, Mr. Clancy," Jack said with a nod.

"All right," Clancy said, fuming. "Be off with you, you bastard foreigners."

Clancy's men watched the Marauders as they climbed into the jeep and drove off.

"What's up, Dad?" Tommy asked.

"We're going to negotiate with the Woodses tonight," Thomas replied.

"You're kidding," his brother, Ryan, said with a gasp.

"Of course, I am," Clancy said confidentially. "We're

going to attend a meeting with those godless heathens and, after finding where they've hidden our cargo, blast them from here to kingdom come."

The Clancys laughed and hugged each other before returning to the house.

In the jeep, on the way back to town, Buddha Chan massaged his round, shaved head. "If we're going to win out here," he muttered, "why do I feel so shitty?"

"Because we've gotten to know the people," Jack said.

"People we're going to lead to slaughter," Mamudi rejoined.

"Yeah, but they're *assholes,*" Kinski insisted.

"They're still people," Jack said.

"Think of it this way," Kinski said. "Remember the old movie *Them*? It was about these giant, nuked-out ants. I caught it on the boob tube when I was on R and R. These little ants get real fucked up and grow into tractor-sized jobs. They start tearing up people and houses and all kinds of things.

"So the good guys have to go in and take out these ants, right? Before they can breed and destroy civilization. Not one of them said, 'Hey, I *like* ants' or 'Hey, it's not the *ants*' fault.' The ants were the enemy and they took them out.

"That's what we have here. These people have gotten so twisted, they're like mutants. If we don't take them out, they can screw up all of Europe. They'll continue to feed off the FSE and the whole world will wind up being controlled by Maximov. When you look at them, try not to see them as people. They're *less* than people."

Mamudi ran a slim finger along his zipper scar. "That doesn't quite cut it, Kinski."

Kinski lapsed into silence. He pulled out his pocket comb and, as the jeep bounced over pothole after pothole, adjusted his hair. "Okay. How about this? Who remembers the old flick *Planet of the Apes*?"

TWENTY-FOUR

As a brazen winter's dusk fell, the Marauders positioned themselves in front of the tiny pub, Barney's. Crazy Jack checked his watch. It was near seven. No sign of either side as yet.

"Do you think they'll fuck up?" Kinski asked nervously.

"No," Jack replied. "They have *honor* at stake. They have *causes* at stake."

"They have *power* at stake," slender Mamudi mumbled, slipping his skull-and-crossboned orb into his empty eye. "They'll be here, but not before the appointed time. Believe me, when all else is lost, a man's pride is the only thing he has left to cling to."

Buddha Chan perched his glasses on the tip of his upturned nose. "I wish you would stop philosophizing."

Mamudi shrugged. "In death there is rebirth."

Buddha nudged him. "Well, could you keep the newborn squalling to a minimum? Some of us still have to be practical."

Mamudi flashed an "okay" smile to Buddha. The rotund Mongol offered a warm bow.

At exactly seven P.M., a horde of vehicles roared up to the front of Barney's Inn, each jockeying for position. The Clancys, in their pickup trucks, narrowly edged out the Woods clan in whatever vehicles they could muster and reached the building first.

Armed men from both families tumbled from the autos, almost racing each other to the front of the pub.

"Check your weapons, gentlemen," Jack announced. "You are both here to talk, not to shoot."

All the men allowed themselves to be frisked by the Marauders. They laid down their arms on a massive table set up outside the front door of the establishment.

The family members were the last to enter.

A very proud William Woods laid down his shotgun in front of the four freedom fighters. "This is all I have, lads," he intoned. "But if you must frisk me, you must."

The Marauders patted him down in the most efficient of fashions.

The Clancys, all five of them, then marched up to the entrance.

"Frisk us all and get it over with," Thomas announced, throwing down a Uzi.

The Marauders did just that. All the Clancys proved clean.

"Step inside," Crazy Jack said.

The men marched inside the pub.

The Marauders, after carefully surveying the area outside the inn, marched inside, weapons held high, and secured the door.

Thomas Clancy and William Woods sat across from each other at the main table.

"So," Clancy said, "what do you have to say to me?"

"Well," Woods offered, "I was thinking about a truce."

"A truce?" Clancy asked. "Why now? Why not ten or twenty years ago?"

"Things have changed," Woods continued. "It's not the same world anymore."

"Damn right," Clancy rejoined.

"We now have a common enemy," Woods continued.

"And who might that be?" Clancy asked.

"Why, the new king of England. He's out to do us all in, I'd venture."

"And if he isn't?" Clancy replied.

William Woods was taken aback. "Well, of course he is. He's out to destroy us."

Clancy smiled. "I might not be believing that."

"But he's a Scot," Woods bellowed. "He knows nothing of the troubles."

"But he's a king," Clancy countered, "and surely you'll be wanting to be on your best behavior to impress your precious new king."

"He's no king of mine," Woods sputtered. "He's a puppet."

"Now we're getting to the point," Clancy said enthusiastically. "And whose puppet is he?"

"Why...," Woods began. "Why, I don't know!"

"Here's what I'm thinking. You're afraid that new king of yours won't be strong enough to take on the Federated States, and you know that the Federated boys are on my side up here. You're stuck between a rock and a hard place, William."

"Are you daft?"

"You might as well tell me where the arms are, you bastard." Clancy was seething. "You can't run afoul of the FSE."

Woods was stunned. "I know that," he said with a scowl, "but wait a minute. How do *you* know that?"

Clancy smiled, his barrel chest heaving with pride. "Because *I'm* representing the FSE around here."

"The hell you are!" Woods bellowed. "The FSE is behind *my* cause."

The two men eyeballed each other and realized both were telling the truth.

An icy tingle slashed through both their spines.

They'd been duped, and they knew it.

Yet there was still enough rivalry for both of them to utter the cry "Now!"

Their respective assassins reached beneath the tables and ran into the men's stalls to retrieve their weapons.

Shocked, all the men returned empty-handed.

"Let me help you out on this," a voice said from high above their heads.

Ian O'Malley, chief FSE goon in the area, stood smiling, Jimmy Cagney-like, from the second floor. He had twelve stolid Eastern European guards flanking him.

"Open up," he said, grinning. *"Now!"*

The Clancy clan made a move for the door.

The solid *budda-budda-budda* screams of AK-47s echoed through the pub.

Thomas was the first to fall, his spine leaping forth from his turned back.

Brothers Ryan and Sean were the next to go, clutching at their necks as their heads left their bodies.

Badly frightened sons Tommy and Jack tried to crawl beneath the tables of the pub as hot lead, shards, and splinters shattered their insides.

Several of Woods's men found their brains on the front wall as they made a move to rush the FSE assassins.

After a moment all was quiet.

William Woods stood in the middle of the pub, shaking. He had pissed in his pants.

Ian O'Malley, a cocky grin spread wide across his face, looked down on the man.

"You *are* a moron," the short, thin man said from above, dancing around.

"You *played* us for fools." Woods was steaming.

"No," O'Malley replied. "You played yourself for fools. I merely aimed you idiots in each other's direction. It was like a puppet show, Woods. And me working the strings all along. Now I want to know who has the arms shipment?"

"I—I swear to God," Woods stammered, "I d-don't know."

"You're probably telling the truth." Little O'Malley went on dancing. "And now I'm finally sure who *does* know."

He and his men trained their weapons on the startled Marauders.

"Hello, Jack." O'Malley grinned. "I thought I had killed you off a long time ago."

"How do you know Jackie?" Woods asked.

"Tsk, tsk. William Woods, you are an idiot. Feast your eyes upon the four Yanks who freed England from the Federated States of Europe."

Woods gaped at the Marauders.

"You've been duped, William," O'Malley said. "And now it's time to settle several scores. Let's go back to your home, shall we? And we'll put all the pieces together."

O'Malley danced down the stairs. "And who knows? If things work out all right, I might even let you live. You can claim a great and glorious victory for your cause and continue to jump when I snap my fingers."

Mamudi, Jack, Buddha Chan, and Kinski swallowed hard, in unison, as O'Malley's goons walked toward them, AK-47s held at waist level.

"Disarm our friends here," O'Malley said with a chuckle.

The guards walked up to the Marauders and pushed them back and forth like sacks of potatoes. The Marauders had their guns yanked out of their hands. They were frisked, and then tossed onto the floor.

"On your feet, heroes." O'Malley grinned.

Jack, Mamudi, Buddha, and Kinski stood slowly. The barrels of the guards' guns followed their every move.

They were dead men now.

They knew it.

TWENTY-FIVE

William Woods sat in his living room in silence. His injured son, Willy, was still sprawled on the couch, his face now resembling a fleshy question mark.

"What's going on, Papa?" he muttered.

"Be quiet, lad." Woods sighed, the fight taken out of him.

Two large guards stood across from them, their weapons trained on father and son.

From outside the home the sounds of a solid beating being administered could be heard. A dull *thwap, thwap, thwap*, followed by a howl of pleasure from O'Malley.

William Woods couldn't see what was going on. One of the FSE goons had parked the Marauders' jeep directly next to the house.

As the beating progressed, O'Malley seemed to grow less pleased.

Finally he did nothing but curse.

The entire time William Woods never heard one of the Marauders cry out in pain.

After a time the beating stopped.

The Marauders were dragged into the Woods's living room, bruised, bleeding, and hog-tied. They were unceremoniously tossed onto the floor. Willy found himself staring in horror at the nearly maimed four men. His father averted his gaze.

"Oh," O'Malley said to William, "you don't like the sight of blood, eh? Well, Mr. Woods, you've certainly spilled enough of it in your time to qualify for vampire status."

O'Malley bounced on the balls of his feet above the Marauders. "I'm losing my patience with you," he said.

"So why not just kill us?" Kinski asked.

"In death there is rebirth," Mamudi mumbled, his glass orb knocked out of his hollow eye socket.

Buddha Chan sighed. "I liked you better before you were religious."

"Shut up!" O'Malley shouted. "I'll kill you, all right, but not when you expect it, and *not* until I get some information!"

"The capital of New Jersey is Trenton," Jack offered from between badly split lips.

O'Malley calmly pulled out a TEC-9 semiautomatic and sent a round slamming into Jack's tethered left arm. The bullet entered just below the shoulder and went on to embed itself in the floor. Jack emitted a low growl.

Mamudi, Chan, and Kinski winced. "You slimy little son of a bitch," Kinski whispered.

"Didn't catch that, hero," O'Malley said, "which is probably just as well."

He sat down on a chair directly in front of the Marauders. Jack was losing a lot of blood. He was still conscious, however, his forehead covered with sweat.

"Now I *know* you've absconded with that arms shipment, just as I know you've been operating up here for a week. And how, you might well wonder, did Ian O'Malley figure out that there were four highly trained mercenaries up here mucking around with things?"

"The FSE has spies everywhere," William Woods offered helpfully. "They're a very knowledgeable bunch."

"Don't try sucking up to me, William," O'Malley said. "You were as easily duped as Clancy by these boys. Frankly, I was expecting more from you. You've always struck me as having a great potential for evil."

Woods was about to smile, but when he realized that the compliment was actually an insult, he slid lower in his chair.

"Well, seeing as how you won't live to tell anybody

about it," O'Malley said, "I'll let you know how you were caught. Luck. Sheer luck. We picked up a young lass on the road, a lass from this very village."

He glanced at Willy. "I believe you know her. Molly McGuire. She was very cooperative."

"Was?" Willy said.

"Oh, yes. I had a lot of fun with her. She told me about how four brave men had rescued her from her prison. Described them to a tee. A fine piece of ass, she was, Willy. You were a fool to let her get away."

"Did you . . . ," Willy asked, his face reddening.

"Did I? Of course I did, and when I was done, I gave her over to my friends here. She pleased them all, although I have to admit that Ivan over here had to settle for something resembling necrophilia."

"You bastard," Jack muttered. "You better pray to God none of us lives through this, or I'll personally rip your head off your syphilitic little body."

O'Malley casually got up and kicked Jack in his wounded arm. Jack gritted his teeth and rolled over on his side, his arms and legs still bound behind the small of his back.

"Anyhow, it didn't take too much figuring out on my part to suss out what you were doing up here. Especially since people in the area had been talking about how the Woodses and the Clancys were upping each other's body count on a daily basis."

O'Malley eased himself back down into his chair. "Now, you know and I know that Maximov wants you dead. He also wants those guns. Now, I could chat with you boys all day. I could also torture you all day. More than likely you'd die before you'd tell me a word, am I right?"

"Damn straight," Buddha Chan said, peering out from behind his shattered glasses.

"I figured as much." O'Malley nodded. "Now, I could threaten to kill Mr. Woods over here, but you probably wouldn't much care. I could do the same to his son, and it still wouldn't have much of an impact, would it?"

Willy Woods glared at O'Malley. "Would you mind if I went outside? I think I'm going to be sick."

O'Malley smiled at the skinny young boy. "All the fire and brimstone knocked out of you, eh?"

He stared at the boy's torn-up, bandaged legs. "Fine. On one condition. You go outside by yourself."

"I can't walk," Willy said.

"Then crawl," O'Malley replied.

Willy Woods slid off the sofa, wincing. Slowly, laboriously, he crawled toward the side door of the house. His father made a move to help him. O'Malley trained his pistol on him. "Let him crawl, Mr. Woods."

Willy slowly slithered up to the side door, barely being able to grasp the doorknob. He gave the doorknob a mighty yank and swung open the portal. Willy Woods pitched forward into the darkness.

O'Malley sat in the living room, giggling like an idiot. He returned his attention to the Marauders.

"Ah, but that's only the *beginning* of tonight's entertainment," he said with a smile. "Wait until you see what's behind door number two."

TWENTY-SIX

One of O'Malley's men dragged old Addled Andrew through the front door and threw him onto the floor directly next to the hog-tied Marauders.

The old man had been beaten. One eye was swollen shut. The few teeth he had remaining in his mouth had been knocked or ripped out. Blood dribbled from his mouth, mingling with the hair of his long white beard.

"Hello, boys," he wheezed, hitting the ground.

"What do you want this old man for?" Kinski groused. "He's just the town character."

"Oh, you're quite a character, aren't you, Andrew?" O'Malley said. "We did a little bit of checking on Andrew, here. He's a bit of a sea man. In fact, he used to be pals with old Mr. McGuire, isn't that right, Andrew?"

"A fine man he was," Andrew said. "If you live an entire lifetime, you'll never be as good as his little toe."

"And Andrew and Mr. McGuire were friends with the old-timers who worked the piers and the docks and, well, you get my point, boys." O'Malley grinned.

He pulled up his TEC-9 and fired a slug into Addled Andrew's right leg. The old man howled in pain. "I don't know anything!" he screeched.

The Marauders exchanged startled glances.

"Now, boys," O'Malley continued, "I know you had to have outside help on this little coup. You didn't get the information from the Clancys, and you didn't get it from the Woodses."

Another shot.

Left leg.

What little blood was left in the wizened old man's body was now flowing from his legs.

O'Malley's face hardened. "Personally I have nothing against Andrew, here. Reminds me of my sainted grand-dad."

He fired a shot into Andrew's left arm.

"But here's the deal, suckers. Unless one of you tells me where you stashed the arms, the next bullet goes through the old son of a bitch's head."

"All right, all right," Crazy Jack moaned.

"Jackie, don't," Andrew said.

"No, Andrew. It's all right. You wanted to die in a peaceful land, right?"

"That I did. . . ."

"Do you promise to let him live?" Jack asked O'Malley.

"You have my word." O'Malley nodded.

The other three Marauders tensed their bodies.

"The guns are hidden in a wooded area directly behind where Woods hid the McGuire girl."

"Thank you, Jack," O'Malley said, sending a bullet smashing into the old man's head, killing him instantly. Bits of skull and brain matter slithered across the wooden floor of William Woods's living room.

O'Malley grinned at Jack. "I lied."

Jack managed a grimace. "So did I."

O'Malley stiffened. "You *what*?"

"You never intended to let the old man live," Jack said, chuckling. "Never kid a kidder, O'Malley."

"I could kill you for that!" O'Malley said.

"Go ahead, and then explain to Maximov how you couldn't find the cargo," Jack said.

O'Malley sank into a chair. "Now," Jack said, "if I were a betting man, and I'm sure you are, ferret face, I'd untie us all and get my arm patched up."

"And why should I do that?"

"Because I'm betting that the only way you're going to get that cargo is if we take you there ourselves."

"That's crazy."

"Life is like that. Now, my arm is hurting me terribly, so *move* it."

O'Malley reluctantly signaled to two guards, "Untie them."

He thought hard. "Those two, toss them over there."

The guards tossed Buddha and Mamudi onto the floor. "You," he ordered Woods, "wrap a towel or something around that asshole's arm."

Woods did as he was told, first pouring some whiskey over Jack's gaping wound.

"You have any gasoline around here?" O'Malley asked Woods.

"Around back—some kerosene for the lanterns."

"Get it."

Moments later Wood returned with several large cans of kerosene.

"Put it over there," O'Malley said, pointing to a spot near the two guards watching Chan and Mamudi.

"You two," O'Malley continued, motioning his weapon toward Jack and Kinski. "Get over to the front door."

O'Malley faced his guards. "Half of you come with us, the other half stay here and keep the home fires burning."

O'Malley smiled at Jack.

"Now," O'Malley said, "if *you* are a betting man, and I'm sure you are, shit-for-brains, you're not going to pull any stunts on me en route to the cargo . . . because if you do, your two friends over here are going to burn alive."

"And suppose I do as I'm told?" Jack asked.

"You'll all die quickly," O'Malley said.

Jack and Buddha exchanged looks. Jack turned to O'Malley.

"Come on, then," O'Malley said, leading Jack, Kinski, and a half dozen guards out of the house. "We'll take one of the trucks."

O'Malley caught a slight movement out of the corner of his eye. "What's that?" he said, noticing a bush quivering.

"House cat," Jack said, suppressing a smile. "Are you coming or what?"

Jack exchanged a quick glance with Kinski. Kinski was in the know as well.

O'Malley pushed Jack into the shotgun position in the front of the cab. O'Malley slid behind the wheel. In the back of the truck, two guards trained their weapons at the back of Jack's head while the other four guarded Kinski.

"Thanks for the attention, guys." Kinski grinned. "I appreciate it."

"Shut up," a guard said in a heavy Slavic accent.

"Does anyone here like kielbasa?" Kinski asked.

"Shut up."

"Personally I've always found it a little greasy."

With the guards distracted and O'Malley trying to pull the truck out from in front of the Woodses' home, all thoughts of the quivering bush were dismissed.

Soon O'Malley and his prisoners were on their way out of town.

Inside the Woods living room, six guards stared at Woods, Buddha, and Mamudi.

A scraping noise could be heard from outside the house.

"What is that?" a guard muttered.

One man walked toward the front door.

"Hey, you bastards!" Willy Woods cried. "It's me! Open up the goddamn door! I can't budge it. It's my legs. Come on, come on, you dick heads, I'm freezing out here!"

"Fuck you, asshole." The guard laughed, training his AK-47 at the center of the closed door. He opened up on the wooden portal, splintering it in the middle.

"Willy!" Woods cried, getting to his feet.

"Sit down," a guard ordered.

A sickened Woods slid back down into his chair.

The snickering sharpshooter guard decided to see how much damage he had done to Willy. He walked over to the bullet-riddled door and swung it open, smiling.

"This is for Molly McGuire, Ivan!" came a voice from below him.

There, on the cold earth some three feet from the door, Willy lay, his shattered legs still useless, cradling Jack's RPG-2 rocket launcher in his arms. The guard was caught by surprise. He hesitated a split second too long in bringing his weapon down in Willy's direction.

Buddha Chan and Mamudi, spotting the tip of the rocket

between the guard's legs, dived to the ground as Willy let go with a whooshing 40-mm shell.

The shell slammed through the first guard's genitalia before roaring into the house. The kerosene at the other guards' feet went up immediately, as did the entire rear wall of the living room.

"Let's move it!" Buddha yelled, scooping up a startled Mr. Woods into his arms and heading for the front door. They leapt over the dead first guard and skittered around a singed but smiling Willy. Mamudi stooped and carried Willy to the curb as the Woods home went up in flames.

From inside could be heard the pathetic shrieking of the five burning FSE goons.

"Has a nice ring to it," Buddha said with a sigh.

Mamudi eased the rocket launcher out of the trembling Willy's hands. "Nice shooting."

The boy nodded mutely.

"I'm proud of you, son," Mr. Woods said, putting an arm around his boy.

"You should be," Willy said, wheezing. "It was a hell of a crawl from the house to that jeep and back again."

Mamudi left Willy and ran to the jeep for a new eye, his SEAL insignia. "Mr. Woods, are you about done with the infighting now?"

Woods nodded wearily, hugging his boy. "My son here had the right idea a few days back, but I wouldn't hear none of it."

"Are you finished dicking around now?" Buddha Chan asked.

"Yes, yes, those FSE bastards are worse than the Nazis themselves," Woods muttered.

"We don't have much time," Mamudi said, sliding into his jeep. "We'll have to round up as many men from town as possible."

"Shouldn't be too hard," Woods said, easing his injured son into the front seat of his station wagon. "Both Catholics and Protestants were killed tonight. The only blood that matters now is Irish. We have to prevent any more from being shed."

"Let's move out," Buddha said, getting into the jeep.

Woods watched Mamudi and Buddha head off toward the main street of the village.

"They're not bad for foreigners," he said, turning the engine over and following suit.

Willy sat next to his father and laughed.

For the first time in a very, very long time he actually *liked* the old man.

TWENTY-SEVEN

Jack rode in silence in the front seat of the farm truck, O'Malley behind the wheel.

Jack's arm hurt like hell. He'd make O'Malley pay for that and for Molly McGuire and for Addled Andrew.

And pay O'Malley, he would.

Jack had seen Willy Woods in the bushes with the rocket launcher. If the kid's aim had been anything more than awful, Buddha and Mamudi had probably turned the situation around by now.

They'd be speeding toward Londonderry cross-country. Jack was content to slow O'Malley down as much as possible on the roadway.

"Cut off your lights and slow it down up here," Jack cautioned.

"Why?"

"We found a group of scavenger sappers out here the other day. We hit two, but I have no idea how many more there were. Tell the goons out back to keep a sharp lookout."

"Scavengers?"

"You're not the only one interested in turning a profit out of plunder," Jack said.

O'Malley muttered a few choice words but did as he was told. He cut his speed by half and drove in darkness for a few miles. He was growing irritated at the constant delays.

"Oh, fuggit," he said, turning the headlamps back on and barreling full tilt toward the Londonderry docks.

The truck pulled into the loading area shortly thereafter. The docks were dark and deserted.

"We'll have to go the rest of the way on foot," Jack said.

"And why's that?" O'Malley asked.

"This place hasn't been used regularly since before the last war; half of the planks here are rotted. However, if you want to take your truck scuba diving, that's fine with me."

"All right, all right," O'Malley said.

"We had to belly-lug everything," Kinski said. "You can handle it."

"I won't be belly-lugging *any*thing," O'Malley replied, glowing with superiority. "We'll just call for reinforcements and get a barge up here, float the stuff right back out again."

"What a clever guy," Kinski said to Jack.

The Marauders were ordered out of the truck. The six FSE goons were at their backs, O'Malley on their right flank. The wind above them howled like harpies. The sea roared.

Kinski heard a tiny, grating sound. Something was bouncing off the planks on the dock. Something was rolling. Like a marble or a stone.

He glanced at his right foot.

Or a glass eye.

He breathed a sigh of relief. "It's down here, O'Malley," he said.

"No tricks now," O'Malley cautioned.

"I'm too tired for tricks," Kinski replied.

The Marauders walked down a deserted alleyway that stretched between two groups of wooden warehouses.

Jack held his injured arm as he hobbled along, his ankles still swollen from the hog-tying.

Kinski's wrists and ankles were swollen as well, but he was buoyed by the fact that Buddha and Mamudi were somewhere nearby.

"You know what I can't understand, O'Malley?" he ventured.

"What's that?"

Jack caught a movement out of his left eye. Shadow-shapes. Several of them. His chest tightened.

"Why do you have to be so over-the-top about everything? What was it, bad toilet training?" Kinski continued.

"Don't tempt me," O'Malley said, seething.

"I mean, why is it you have to hot-dog everything. You can't just get a job done, you have to take unnecessary chances, kill more than you have to. It's like the old Special Forces a couple of decades ago. They went from an elite group to a bunch of cowboys. You'd get a lot more accomplished if you thought before you acted."

"Spare me the sermon," O'Malley said.

"I can't figure out," Jack said, "why you had to shoot old Addled Andrew. He was a harmless old soul. He just wanted to die in a quiet country, a quiet, peaceful man. Why did you have to brutalize him like that, slaughter him like that?"

"Maybe it's because I don't like useless old men. Does that satisfy ya?" O'Malley smirked.

"Don't tell me." Jack shrugged. "Tell them."

Jack dived to the right and Kinski to the left, leaving O'Malley and his six goons standing in the middle of the alleyway. Jack was immediately pulled inside one warehouse and Kinski into another. Then the alleyway was filled with blazing lights.

There were two trucks blocking the FSE unit's path.

The goons opened fire with their AK-47s, shattering the headlights and plunging O'Malley into darkness.

"What's going on here?" he demanded.

The goons pivoted wildly, scanning fore and aft as well as above.

"What's going on here?" O'Malley shrieked.

By way of an answer, the air around him erupted with dozens of tiny pinpricks of light and thunder.

Muzzle flashes danced around O'Malley's men's heads.

Within seconds they were down.

The hidden assailants continued to fire, ripping the FSE guards' bodies to shreds.

O'Malley felt a powerful arm grab him around the throat. Crazy Jack Keenan yanked the wiry little man high off the ground. Still clutching his 9-mm gun in his right hand, O'Malley tried to break Jack's hold with his left.

"In answer to your question, O'Malley," Jack hissed, "this is payback."

"I'll take that, thank you," Buddha Chan said, waddling out of the darkness in front of O'Malley and gingerly picking up the gun.

"Long time no see, and only partially at that," Mamudi said, reappearing.

Kinski walked out, with a hobbling Willy Woods at his side. "Hate to spoil the party, runt, but young Willy here got your other men really burned up."

William Woods and a full thirty men from the village emerged from two warehouses. Inside the warehouses was stored the infamous cargo.

O'Malley's eyes grew wide with terror. There were both Woods supporters and Clancy supporters in the ranks.

"You wound up doing us all a big favor, Mr. O'Malley," Woods said, smiling. "You've managed to do in a single evening what England and dozens of church leaders and politicians have been trying to do for more than a century. You've brought us together. Now, how about that?"

"You're insane," O'Malley hissed from between clenched teeth.

"Maybe so," Woods said with a nod. "But it's a good feeling, you know that? Maybe there will never be one Ireland, but there'll always be one people. You know where you went wrong, you weasel? People have dreams that may never come true, but if you promise people dreams, then eventually they're going to want them to come true. And if you hold out on that delivery, well, the people get mad, and then they turn against those who are playing with their dreams."

"Let me put it to you in terms you'll understand, you bastard," Willy said. "You promise a dog a treat long enough, you better give him one or he'll bite your ass off. Oh, yeah. I have a present for you."

Mamudi led him up to a dangling O'Malley. He stuffed something cool and wet down O'Malley's pants.

Jack let go of O'Malley, allowing the man to tumble onto the ground. "What *is* this?" O'Malley said hoarsely.

"Ivan's balls," Willy said.

"And now," Jack said, "we're going to leave you here. We have to pack up the cargo and get it back to the village. King Shatterhand should be here soon. He'll be expecting to take this back with him. He has divisions in both Belfast and Dublin that are looking forward to meeting you."

"You're not going to kill me?" O'Malley asked.

"No," Jack said, "but we're not going to save you either."

"From what?"

"Oh, you know, wharf rats? Useless old men?"

The Marauders and the men of Feirgall turned their backs on O'Malley and closed the warehouse doors shut.

O'Malley was left, crouched and gasping, in the center of the darkened alleyway.

Silence.

O'Malley tensed.

There was someone nearby. He could sense it.

Then he heard it: footsteps.

All around him.

He skittered to his feet, nose running, throat sore, eyes tearing. "Who's there?" he whimpered.

"Just a few friends of Andrew's" came a voice from the mist.

"You remember Andrew, don't you?" echoed a second.

"You didn't have to do that to him, did you?" came a third voice.

O'Malley gazed into the murkiness before him. Shadows shambled forward. Short and squat. Lean and tall. Their gait was affected by the cold and the damp, but their hearts were determined.

O'Malley whirled toward the dock's end. If he could make it to the water, he'd have a chance.

Had to make it to the water.

A large plank slammed into his right leg, just below the kneecap.

O'Malley shrieked, feeling the bones splinter.

"How did it feel to slowly drain the life from an old man?" came another voice. "Did it make you feel *big*? Did it make you feel powerful?"

"Fuck you," O'Malley muttered.

He hopped on, on one leg, using the warehouse walls to prop himself up.

A massive work shoe sliced forward out of the mist, slamming into his left ankle.

O'Malley felt his ankle snap. His foot turned over on its side.

He'd crawl. He'd crawl for the water.

"Did you get enjoyment out of placing bullets into limb after limb?" asked the mist.

O'Malley slithered on the damp dock, like a slime-encased slug.

A pointed plank sliced into his flesh just above his right elbow.

"And when you put the final bullet in his brain," said the night, "did you think of it as a grand and glorious *joke*?"

O'Malley was bleating now, whimpering like a small, feral creature.

"Get away from me, you bastards."

His good left hand found a piling at dock's end. He pulled himself up into a standing position. There was a small boat below. If he could reach it . . . If only he could reach it.

"Does *this* strike you as being funny?" cackled the night.

O'Malley lunged for freedom.

He felt the flat side of a large metal hook smash against the backside of his skull.

His body seemed to convulse.

He clawed the air with his good hand.

He tried to kick his legs free of the dock.

His legs weren't working anymore.

He found himself tumbling awkwardly through the cold night air.

His face collided with the water, forcing the air out of his lungs and causing him to gag.

He took a deep breath.

No air entered his throat.

Only dank, dark water.

He spotted the small boat not two feet before him.

He raised his good hand.

Then . . . darkness.

On the edge of the dock far above, Addled Andrew's friends stood, gazing into the pitch-black sea.

"Should we use a gun to finish the puny little dick off?" said one to the other.

"No," a second answered. "Let him suffer."

"More food for the fish," said a third.

The elderly men turned and walked to the warehouses. There was still a lot of work to do that evening.

TWENTY-EIGHT

Shatterhand's troops swept up into the area less than three days later. Their march northward had been successful. Shatterhand had promised individual freedom and a new era of tolerance for all, and the war-weary people seemed to want just that.

In Feirgall, the Marauders allowed Shatterhand to bask in the spotlight and share the goodwill of the people.

They found themselves drawn to the docks of Londonderry more often than not.

And it was on a cold, crisp morning that they witnessed the old dockworkers burying their good friend Addled Andrew from a barge not a mile out of the harbor.

They watched the old men lower the canvas-encased cadaver into Andrew's beloved sea.

"I liked that man," Jack said.

"Me too." Kinski nodded, the wind mussing up his well-done locks for the umpteenth time.

"He was a simple man," Buddha said with a nod, "yet strong in the courage of his convictions."

Mamudi nodded. "Although there are but five musical notes," he said, "in combination the melodies are too numerous to be heard. There are not more than five primary colors, but in combination they produce more colors than could ever be seen. There are not more than five basic tastes, yet they yield more flavors than could ever be tasted."

He turned to his companions. "Sun Tzu said that twenty-five hundred years ago. Addled Andrew *lived* that truth. In simplicity there is variety and strength."

The Marauders nodded.

"I'm not as eloquent as you, Freddie," Jack said. "But I do know *one* Irish saying that I think old Andrew would have enjoyed."

He watched Andrew's corpse bob for a few seconds before sinking below the waves. "May joy and peace surround you, contentment latch your door. And may happiness be with you now, and bless you evermore."

"Amen," Buddha added.

The Marauders turned from the dockside and headed back to their jeep.

"Guess we should head out," Jack said.

"It's a long drive south," Buddha added.

"Should be all right." Kinski shrugged. "For the next two months all we have to do is secure Shatterhand's garrisons. It's more of a goodwill mission than anything else."

"You never can tell what'll happen," Jack muttered.

The four men climbed in the jeep, Buddha behind the wheel. He turned the engine over.

"They never did find a trace of O'Malley's body," he said.

"I know," Jack said.

"Who cares?" Kinski said.

"He may still be alive," Mamudi said.

"I hope he is," Jack said grinning.

"Why's that?" Mamudi asked.

"As long as we have a bad guy we can picture in our minds," Jack said, leaning back in the seat, "we have someone to fight against."

Mamudi laughed aloud. "You are indeed a wise man, Jack Keenan."

"Bullshit," Jack said. "I'm just a soldier."

Buddha swiveled the jeep around and headed out from Londonderry.

Within minutes a wave of early-morning fog engulfed the jeep, erasing it from view.

None of the men on the funeral barge noticed its passing.

It was as if the Marauders had never been there.

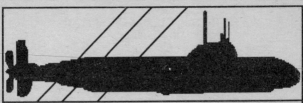

Tom Clancy's

#1 NEW YORK TIMES BESTSELLERS

— **THE HUNT FOR RED OCTOBER**   0-425-08383-7/$5.50
"The Perfect Yarn."—President Ronald Reagan
"A fine thriller... flawless authenticity, frighteningly genuine."—*The Wall Street Journal*

— **RED STORM RISING**   0-425-10107-X/$5.95
"Brilliant...staccato suspense."—*Newsweek*
"Exciting...fast and furious."—*USA Today*

— **PATRIOT GAMES**   0-425-10972-0/$5.50
"Elegant...A novel that crackles."—*New York Times*
"Marvelously tense...He is a master of the genre he seems to have created."—*Publishers Weekly*

— **THE CARDINAL OF THE KREMLIN** 0-425-11684-0/$5.95
"The best of the Jack Ryan series!"—*New York Times*
"Fast and fascinating!"—*Chicago Tribune*
